T0034453

The God of Nishi-Yuigahama Station

Takeshi Murase

YEN ON

New York

The God of Nishi-Yuigahama Station

TAKESHI MURASE

Translation by Giuseppe di Martino
Cover art by Pochi

This book is a work of fiction. Names, characters, places, and incidents are the product of the author's imagination or are used fictitiously. Any resemblance to actual events, locales, or persons, living or dead, is coincidental.

NISHIYUIGAHAMAEKI NO KAMISAMA
©Takeshi Murase 2020
First published in Japan in 2020 by KADOKAWA CORPORATION, Tokyo.
English translation rights arranged with KADOKAWA CORPORATION, through TUTTLE-MORI AGENCY, INC., Tokyo.

English translation © 2024 by Yen Press, LLC

Yen Press, LLC supports the right to free expression and the value of copyright. The purpose of copyright is to encourage writers and artists to produce the creative works that enrich our culture.

The scanning, uploading, and distribution of this book without permission is a theft of the author's intellectual property. If you would like permission to use material from the book (other than for review purposes), please contact the publisher. Thank you for your support of the author's rights.

Yen On
150 West 30th Street, 19th Floor
New York, NY 10001

Visit us at yenpress.com • facebook.com/yenpress • twitter.com/yenpress
yenpress.tumblr.com • instagram.com/yenpress

First Yen On Edition: May 2024
Edited by Yen On Editorial: Rachel Mimms
Designed by Yen Press Design: Wendy Chan

Yen On is an imprint of Yen Press, LLC.
The Yen On name and logo are trademarks of Yen Press, LLC.

The publisher is not responsible for websites (or their content) that are not owned by the publisher.

Library of Congress Cataloging-in-Publication Data
Names: Murase, Takeshi, author. | Di Martino, Giuseppe, 1989– translator.
Title: The god of Nishi-Yuigahama Station / Takeshi Murase ; translation by
    Giuseppe di Martino.
Other titles: Nishiyuigahamaeki no kamisama. English
Description: First Yen On edition. | New York : Yen On, 2024.
Identifiers: LCCN 2024000539 | ISBN 9781975392024 (hardcover)
Subjects: CYAC: Railroad accidents—Fiction. | Ghosts—Fiction. | LCGFT:
    Ghost stories. | Fantasy fiction. | Light novels.
Classification: LCC PZ7.1.M838 Go 2024 | DDC [Fic]—dc23
LC record available at https://lccn.loc.gov/2024000539

ISBNs: 978-1-9753-9202-4 (hardcover)
        978-1-9753-9203-1 (ebook)

10 9 8 7 6 5 4 3 2 1

LSC-C

Printed in the United States of America

CONTENTS

One early spring day in Kamakura, when the storm winds were signaling winter's end, a rapid-service train running inbound on Touhin Railway's Kamakura Line derailed, veering off the tracks at blistering speeds and grazing the torii gate of Kamakura Ikitama Shrine before careening off a cliff and into a ravine. Sixty-eight of the hundred and twenty-seven passengers died in the catastrophic crash.

Around two months following the accident, rumors began to fly that a ghost train was running on the Kamakura Line in the dead of night. The closest station to the crash site was one Nishi-Yuigahama Station. On its platforms resided a spirit named Yukiho—and if one asked her, they could travel back in time and board the train on the day of the accident. However, in order to do so, the following four rules had to be strictly observed:

- You may board the train only from the station where the doomed rider first boarded.
- You mustn't tell the doomed rider that they are soon to die.
- You must get off the train at or before passing Nishi-Yuigahama Station. Otherwise, you, too, shall die in the accident.
- Meeting the doomed rider will not change their fate. No matter what you do, those who died in the accident will not come back to life. If you attempt to get people off the train before it derails, you will be returned to the present day.

Meeting the doomed won't change the present.

No matter what you do, those who died in the tragedy will never come back to life.

But hearing those rules did nothing to deter people from seeing their loved ones.

A woman whose fiancé died. A son whose father died. A junior high school student whose crush died. And the wife of the conductor who caused the derailment.

Invariably, it's only after losing a loved one that people realize how beautiful those days had been—the days that would never return.

If you could see someone you've lost one more time, what would *you* tell them?

CHAPTER 1
TO HIM, I SAY

"The highway is blocked off due to the accident, so I'll be taking a different route, ma'am."

Sitting in the back seat of the cab, I couldn't find any words to say in reply. I saw through the window how choked with crowds of rubberneckers the Nishi-Yuigahama area was. Thanks to the derailment, all trains on the Kamakura Line had stopped operating. As shrill ambulance sirens blared outside, I opened my smartphone while wiping the sweat off my forehead. The accident dominated the headlines across several news sites:

As of 14:00, 26 Dead in Kamakura Derailment

Kamakura Derailment: Car 3 Threatening to Fall Off Cliff

As soon as that avalanche of headlines hit me, I hastily closed the page. Taking a deep breath, I recalled a phone exchange from earlier today.

"Hey, Tomo, honey, sorry to call you at work."

"What's wrong, Mother?"

"Try to take what I'm about to say calmly. The train Shin'ichirou was on just derailed."

"What?"

"Shin'ichirou's train just derailed!"

"Is…is Nemoto okay? Is he all right—?"

"Just come straight to Minami-Kamakura General Hospital. Bye."

I couldn't even tell you how many times I'd turned that conversation over in my mind since getting in this taxi. Her wording. The way she'd been breathing. The pauses in her speech. I combed through everything I'd heard during that call with my mother-in-law, hunting for any possibility my fiancé might conceivably be okay.

The cabbie frowned. "Traffic's bad down this road, too…"

"Please just do what you can!"

Deep down, I didn't actually want him to hurry. I was too scared. The closer that white building loomed, the faster my heart raced. Afraid to face whatever reality awaited me, I would have given anything to go back in time. Any moment in my life would be fine, really, as long as it wasn't this one.

"We've arrived! The front entrance is crowded, so I'll take you to the rear—"

"No, here's fine! Please let me off here!"

I handed him a ten-thousand-yen bill and didn't even wait to receive my change before exiting the car. Keeping the oncoming camera crews off my back with a hand, I crossed the roundabout. A number of police escort buses were parked in front of the hospital's main entrance. They must not have had enough stretchers to go around, because the train seats were being used as makeshift gurneys to carry the wounded inside.

"We'll take care of that patient later! This one comes first!"

Beyond the automatic doors, it was a sea of chaos.

"I told you before, Doctor! This one's higher priority!"

"Listen to me—we're all out of beds! Take the dead to the basement for the time being!"

Shouting rang through the halls, accompanied by the heavy pattering of footsteps as people rushed stretchers here and there and every which way.

Weaving my way through the crowds, I hurried over to reception. "Excuse me, where's Shin'ichirou Nemoto? He was in the derailment today!"

"Are you his next of kin?" the young nurse asked.

"I'm his fiancée!" I told her. "My name's Tomoko Higuchi!"

She ducked into a room in the back, returning to the reception desk after consulting another nurse.

"…Could you please go to Floor B2, to the room toward the back on the right-hand side?"

My heart skipped a beat.

The basement…

I racked my brain in search of what that could mean, feeling more and more dazed and overwhelmed all the while. I took the emergency staircase to B2; the whole floor was a soundscape of sobs. Proceeding down the dim corridor, I heard familiar voices from a room beside the boiler closet and came to a halt, frozen in place with my hand on the doorknob to that room—because I had an idea what sight would greet me on the other side. I closed my eyes and exhaled all the air I'd been holding in the pit of my stomach, riding that momentum to pull the door open.

The scene that came into view was more or less what I'd been picturing. A large bed, a person lying atop it, and a white cloth draped over that person's face.

My head was swimming, my thoughts running amok. Where was I again? What was I doing?

"Tomo!"

My mother-in-law walked up to me and gripped my right hand tightly in her hands.

"Tomo! Tomo, honey! *Tomo!*"

She was in my space. In that moment, she felt like a nuisance to me. The woman was interrupting my ability to sort my thoughts; the urge to brush off her hands was strong. But I couldn't do it. The strength of her vise grip conveyed her love for her only son. Letting go wasn't an option.

"Tomo. You should come look at Shin'ichirou. At his face."

My father-in-law pulled me by the arm. He removed the cloth, and there it was.

Nemoto's face always looked so cute and boyish when he was sleeping. I'd loved watching it as he slept. Once, I'd even stared at it all through the night in bed together.

We were supposed to celebrate his thirty-second birthday next week. He'd asked me to whip him up a nice curry meal for the occasion. When I made him one for his last birthday, he got tears in his eyes as he spooned in mouthfuls. And when I asked why he was crying, he replied:

"It's nothing. I was just thinking, man, I get to eat your curry so many times before I die!"

I was so happy. So, so happy. He was *pure*, the little kid inside him alive and kicking. And I got to be with him. I was so happy I got to spend the rest of my future with this man.

"Wake up, darling. I'm begging you, wake up..." I gripped his hand. "Open your eyes. I'll make you some curry again. I'll make you some every day. So please wake up for me, Nemoto! *Nemoto!*"

My father-in-law rubbed my shoulders, his hands shaking too much for him to hide it. As I cried into his chest, I remembered the moment I first met Nemoto.

It was sixteen years ago, when I was a freshman in high school.

My father suffered from an ailing heart, to the point where he was no longer able to work, and while my mother took his place at the neighborhood's printing factory, life was tough. To help make ends meet, I started working part-time as a caregiver at a local old-age home after school.

One day during the Golden Week string of holidays, I had to go on a field trip to tour an automobile plant for some "extracurricular enrichment." I was walking alone, away from my group; the girl who'd invited me into her group in class hadn't made eye contact with me since we got off the bus. We'd sat next to each other on the way there, and I could tell that I bored her because I wasn't talkative enough for her tastes. She must have decided during the ride that someone as glum as me wasn't worth her time.

Come lunch, we went to eat at the cafeteria attached to the tire factory. The kids who'd brought bento boxes from home had them for lunch, but my mother had been away on a business trip that day, so I didn't have a bento of my own. She'd slipped me some spending money, but given our poor financial situation, I could hardly afford to part with it too readily.

"...I'll have a thing of *kake udon*, please," I said, ordering the cheapest item on the menu.

Then I headed for the long table where the other girls in my group were seated, but I stopped short nearby. They were all smirking meanly as they shot glances my way. One of them even whispered into the next girl's ear loud enough for me to hear:

"Can you believe there's a girl who'd eat something as ghetto as that?"

I did an about-face, their comments stabbing me like a rain of knives to the back. It was the girl who'd invited me into the group who made that remark. She'd put her bag on the chair next to her so that I couldn't sit there.

I took a seat at an empty table. Another student passed me by, a hamburger-steak platter tray in hand. At a table toward the back, a few other kids were relishing their *yakiniku*. I felt wretched. Whenever somebody somewhere was laughing, I felt like they must've been laughing at *me*.

"I'll have some *kake udon*, too, thanks," came one person's voice.

He'll have some, "too"? I turned to look. It was a rather short boy from my class.

He sat down next to me, tray in hand. Without a word to me, he split open his disposable chopsticks and started slurping up his noodles. He had a little kid's big round eyes, as well as a slight tan. He didn't look at me much, probably out of shyness. On those occasions our eyes met, we blinked bashfully and quickly looked away.

It wasn't lost on me——by ordering the same thing that I had, he was shielding me from embarrassment. And he was sitting there to serve as a wall, concealing me from the gazes of the kids nearby as if to say, *I'm the only one eating any plain old* kake udon *here. If you're gonna be snickering, snicker at* me.

Even after he finished eating his udon, he didn't get up from his seat. He didn't get up to refill his now-empty glass, either. He was firmly rooted in place, all to protect me. His kindness struck me right in the heart. As I put my chopsticks in my bowl, I started shuddering from the shoulders. I wiped away the tears rolling down my cheeks and put my lips to my bowl. The soup was a little cold now, but the richness and flavor of the bonito stock suffused me from head to toe.

Shin'ichirou Nemoto was the boy's name.

During lunch two days after the trip, I was eating my bento alone in my classroom. The girls who'd been in the same group as me were sneering at the crude contents of my lunch box. Not feeling terribly welcome there, I went to the library after finishing my meal and happened upon Nemoto there. He was perusing a field guide he'd picked up entitled *How to Train Your Dog*.

I hadn't gotten the chance to thank him yet. When I approached in order to talk to him, that same group of girls crashed the library. Figuring that I'd be fueling the rumor mill if I spoke to him then and there, I left the library to catch him another day, but I got another chance rather quickly: After school, when I took my bike out of the main gate and turned the corner, I saw him. He slipped away from the crowd of students returning home and into the gap between the apartment buildings.

I hit the brakes and peered in. He was walking down the long, narrow drainage channel, splashing noisily as he went. He didn't even roll up the hem of his slacks; clearly, he didn't care they were getting dirty.

I still had over an hour until I was due at my nursing gig. Curious, I decided to follow him. I dipped my sneakered feet into the murky water. After walking down about thirty meters, I stopped sharply—I could see dark-green trees in the distance. I got to the other side of the ditch, where a vast and grand woodland stretched before my eyes, the cedars standing tall like a primeval forest. My home was about a fifteen-minute bike ride from this forest. I'd passed by these woods several times when I was little.

Listening closely, I heard the rustling of trodden undergrowth coming from within the thicket. Nemoto was probably heading deep into the forest. I crossed the small wooden bridge spanning the flume and wrung out the edge of my skirt. Then I stepped up the gentle slope and pushed through the branches and leaves.

When I set foot on an animal trail, I stopped for a breather. Suddenly, I could hear progressively faster and faster footsteps from somewhere. It came like an avalanche down the steep slope and appeared in front of me: a pure-white dog wearing an old yellow collar. Its eyes were bloodshot, and it was glaring at me, clearly about to pounce.

"Eeeeek!"

I fell right on my butt, and Nemoto came running down the slope like a bat out of hell. He wasted no time in standing in front of me to block the way. The hulking canine—it looked like an Akita—charged at us, panting heavily. Nemoto slumped low like a catcher in a baseball match. When the dog came a hairbreadth from his face, he held it back by its lower body and gently turned it to the side in a judo scarf hold. From how calm he seemed, he must have ironed out that series of motions beforehand.

"Sorry 'bout getting rough with ya like that, Shiro. It won't take a minute." Then he shouted my name. "Higuchi! You see my bag there, right? There's a first-aid kit in there, so could ya take it out for me?"

"O-okay, got it," I managed, taken aback as I was. I took the small box out of the bag and walked up to Nemoto. He was lying down.

"This'll be over in a jiffy, Shiro. Hate to bother ya, Higuchi, but could ya put the disinfectant on this foreleg for her? You see the bit on her right elbow where she's bleeding, yeah?"

He pointed at it with his eyes. Sure enough, there was a gash there, about five centimeters wide. The wound was too shallow to need stitches, but the scab was open and still bleeding.

"She'll get germs in the wound if we don't treat it. Just go ahead and dump the whole bottle of disinfectant on there for me."

"Uh, right, got it!"

I bent down next to this barking dog—apparently named "Shiro"—uncapped the little bottle, and sprinkled it over the gash. Her abdomen writhed from the pain, but Nemoto steeled his arms and held her still.

"Thanks. Next, wrap it with some gauze for her."

He gave me instructions one after the other. I wrapped a bandage over the gauze and slipped a brace on top of that. He was treating this dog so conscientiously, you'd think he was administering care to a fellow human.

I did as I was told and zipped up the brace.

"Thanks a ton, Higuchi. Gotta say, I'm glad I learned this move during my judo lessons!"

Sweat beading all over his face, he let go of Shiro's right foreleg. Then he got up and patted the dog on the head.

"Good girl. You did good, Shiro."

The right sleeve of his dress shirt had been torn off, but if that concerned him, he certainly didn't show it.

Shiro sprang to her feet. She was extremely excited and barked a lot until she eventually lost interest and ran off deeper into the woods.

"All that aside, I was wondering who might be tailing me. So that was you the whole time, huh?"

He was panting as he retrieved from his bag a small stainless steel thermos that had an illustration of Snoopy at its center. He poured some of the tea into a cup and gulped it down.

I gave him a quizzical look. "What're you doing here, exactly?"

"These woods've been known as Stray Dogs' Woods for ages. People who can't keep their dogs anymore come dump 'em here. If you go deeper in, you'll see more of 'em." He buttoned up his shirt. "A little bit back, I spotted Shiro wandering near the school's main gate. I couldn't leave her be with her leg injured like that, so I followed her into the forest. But she's a real stubborn gal. I tried feeding her, but she just wouldn't eat."

That must've been why he'd been looking at that dog book in the library. His arms had bite marks and scratches—evidence of the days he'd spent tussling with Shiro.

"By the way, I'm the one who named her Shiro," he said, turning to face the direction the dog had run off in. "I wanna be friends with her. She's just on edge from getting tossed aside like that by humans. I'm sure she's perfectly nice once she gets to know ya," he said with an affectionate gaze, his eyes melancholy but clear. "So anyway, what brings you here?"

"Er, well…," I said timidly. He'd thrown the topic back to me so suddenly. I cleared my throat and looked down at the ground. "The day before yesterday, we went on that field trip, remember? When I sat down to eat that *kake udon*, you sat next to me with some *kake udon* of your own, and I can't tell you how happy that made me. So I thought I'd make today the day I thanked you, since I didn't get a chance to before… Thanks."

I found myself bowing. I raised my head back up, and he didn't reply at all. He was neither embarrassed nor boastful about it. He just smiled reflexively. And I could see the tenderness in his eyes again, same as a moment ago.

"Shiro, c'mere!" Holding a thin, dried cut of meat, he beckoned Shiro. "No need to be scared, Shiro! Come get some beef jerky!"

I followed him. Unfortunately, Shiro didn't come the slightest bit closer.

Over the span of two weeks, the barking had died down. Shiro's foreleg had completely recovered, and she tore off the brace using her teeth. He placed a food bowl in the grassy area Shiro had made her home, filling it with dog food every day. The next day, he'd invariably discover the dog food was completely gone. She was probably eating it, but if he tried feeding her directly, she'd keep her distance.

"Shiro doesn't trust humans, see," he'd told me once. *"Her owner must've treated her horribly."*

The way I saw it, he was probably on the money.

"Tomorrow's Saturday, so I'll hit the pet store and pick their brains about some stuff. See ya next week!"

With that, we went our separate ways for the day; I headed for my part-time work as a caregiver.

Following my forest encounter with Nemoto, I started visiting those woods every weekday after school. We didn't talk too much at school, partially because our seats in class were pretty far apart. But once school was out, we both headed to the forest as we'd arranged beforehand.

Once, when I was walking down the drainage ditch, he appeared behind me and smiled. This sense of distance between us, where we'd go there but not side by side, felt nice for some reason. I was fine with things staying the way they were.

The time I spent with him in the forest became precious to me. Like me, he was an only child. When I opened up to him about my ailing father, he listened to me earnestly. Despite his childlike looks, he was emotionally mature. That group of mean girls at school was cold to me, but thanks to the quality time I was spending with Nemoto, it didn't bother me anymore.

* * *

The entire sky was shrouded in gray, and the rain pattered on the abundant and unruly cedars.

On that day, when the rainy season had officially reached the Kanto region, I was there in the forest. It looked like heavy showers that night, so even Nemoto probably wouldn't be coming. I kept my expectations low, but I went to the forest with an umbrella just in case, and there he was—in a transparent raincoat and about to give Shiro some beef jerky.

"You hungry, Shiro?"

The poor girl was probably in a bad mood after all that rain, making her even more aggressive than usual. Her sopping wet body stiffened, and she barked to intimidate him. Apparently, when training an Akita, it was important to make it clear who the leader was—or so the person at the pet store had told Nemoto, but he wasn't following that advice.

"If you ask me, she's never felt any love from anybody. I don't wanna create a master-servant relationship with her."

He'd declared that without even a hint of doubt, leaving me speechless.

"You don't gotta be afraid, Shiro. Come here. Come eat some."

I watched him from under my plastic umbrella. Shiro wasn't coming any closer. Maybe out of irritation at the intensifying rain, she looked up at the sky and howled. Then as if that was a warning, she lunged at him and bit his right hand.

"Nemoto!"

"It's okay!" he shouted as soon as I called his name.

Shiro still had her teeth in his hand. Despite the anguish on his face, Nemoto's strong sense of purpose hadn't abated from his eyes. Shiro tried to open her mouth, but as if to say, *If you're gonna chew it to shreds, go ahead and do it*, Nemoto made to shove his hand even deeper into it instead.

Shiro moved away, looking displeased. Meanwhile, I was frozen in place with my umbrella. I looked at my watch and realized I was past due for work.

The showdown between the two continued as darkness began to settle over the woods. Whenever Nemoto walked up to Shiro with food, she kept her distance. Whenever Shiro approached to sink her teeth in him, he closed the distance, prompting Shiro to retreat again.

The hands of my watch would soon strike eight. Out of nowhere, the rain grew even heavier, pounding the whole forest. Perhaps frightened by the downpour, Shiro turned her back on Nemoto and ran deeper into the woods. He exhaled through his nose.

Guess we'll leave it at that for today? his eyes said to me.

Just then, a strange wail echoed through the forest. Nemoto started running in the direction that Shiro had gone in, and I ran after him. Suddenly, he stopped. In the direction he was looking lay a large lake that was green with algal blooms. The downpour had caused the water to rise, and legs of pure-white fur were sticking out from under the surface.

"Shiro!"

He took off his raincoat and jumped feetfirst into the lake without checking how deep it was. Using breaststrokes, he swam near the center point and tried to lift Shiro's large frame from below. The water level was just shallow enough; he was able to get her standing, and her face emerged from underwater. However, Shiro became frenzied and started flailing.

Panicking, I spotted a wooden hut. There was a wound-up watering hose next to the door.

That's it!

"Nemoto! Grab on!"

I ran to the shed, unreeled the hose, and threw it into the water. Still holding Shiro, he reached the lake's edge.

"Higuchi!" he called. "Please pull her out first!"

Mustering the kind of superstrength born in times of crisis, I managed to grab Shiro's forelegs and pull her out despite the muddy footing. The water had risen even higher; it now reached Nemoto's nose. He was running out of energy and was starting to move away from the water's edge when he managed to grab the hose. I stooped down and marshaled all my strength to pull him in. Then I slipped on the wet ground and onto my butt, continuing to pull. My arm was giving out, so I held the hose under my left armpit to keep it from slipping away.

"Just run, Higuchi!"

But I kept the hose in place and wrapped it around my right arm.

"Don't let go of the hose, Nemoto!" I cried as he started drifting back out into the lake again. "'Cause if you let go, you're gonna hear it from me!"

I'd never, ever forget what he did for me when I ordered that bowl of *kake udon*. So now it was my turn to save him.

It happened right around when the rain got heavy enough to obscure my vision.

"What's wrong?!" came a voice.

The beam of a flashlight illuminated my face. A middle-aged man with an umbrella had ventured down the same path we had. Shiro ran up to him, barking for him to follow. He rushed over to my side.

"What's the matter? What's wrong?!" he asked me.

"Please save him!"

The man stood in front of me and gripped the hose tight. We continued to reel it in, slipping in the mud the whole time.

Nemoto reached the edge again, and we grabbed him by his hands and lifted him up out of the water bit by bit.

I crouched down to check on him as he lay face down on the ground. "You okay, Nemoto?"

He sat up. "Ha-ha, I'm good. What about you, Higuchi? You hurt?" He was panting, but he seemed fine otherwise. "Don't push yourself too hard."

"You took the words right out of my mouth!"

He flashed a satisfied smile. I chuckled, my expression relaxing.

The man who'd come to our aid told us to take shelter in the nearby hut for the time being. Still soaking wet, we sat down on the eaved veranda.

The man looked appalled. "The hell are you two doing here?! You musta seen the rain advisory!"

Nemoto bowed his head and apologized before summing up the situation.

"By the way, how did you know we were out here?" he asked as he buttoned up his shirt.

The man glanced at the lake. "That white dog kept barking up at our apartment building. It was so loud, I ended up getting an umbrella and going outside. Then it bit the hem of my jeans and took me into the forest. I had no choice but to follow it, and then I saw you two at the lake. That pooch just saved your asses. If you wanna thank anybody, thank that dog over there."

Shiro, who'd been nearby a moment ago, was now at the edge of the lake. The rain was getting weaker. And there she was in the distance, staring at us.

I later found out that the rainfall had broken records that day. Looking back, I think I often went into the forest on days like those.

The next day was a Saturday, so I was considering taking a break during the long weekend. But those hopes were soon dashed when my father died suddenly.

He'd been suffering from worsening angina pectoris and had been in and out of the hospital several times over the past few years. When I woke up in the morning on Sunday, two days after that heavy rain, his body was found cold in his room. Acute heart failure.

It wasn't until after the rushed and hectic funeral was over, once everything had been put away, that the deluge of emotion hit me. Memory after memory of my dad crossed my mind, and I couldn't get out of my futon. After consulting with my mother, I decided to take a short break from school.

A week later, I plucked up the willpower to return to class. When I visited the forest after school that day, Nemoto was nowhere to be found. I headed to the hut, too, on the off chance he was there, but no dice.

There was an inclined road to the west of the lake. It looked man-made, with thin wire ropes on either side. I climbed by holding on to the ropes until I arrived at a small hill. Unlike the disordered trees in the vicinity, this area was neatly segmented. Two glossy log chairs were set up in the back, and near the center was a bright-green lawn with perfectly manicured grass. Who knew such a place existed in that forest?

I heard a rustling; somebody was moving through the brush. I looked down to find Nemoto standing deep amid the long dense grass.

When he noticed me, he asked me over his shoulder, "What, you end up catching a cold?"

"Nah, I'm fine. What about you, Nemoto?" I replied, closing the distance between us.

"I'm fine, too. I may be slender, but I'm surprisingly sturdy."

"Good. Let me tell you, though, my folks yelled at me like there was no tomorrow. 'Where'd you run off to at that ungodly hour without telling us anything?!'"

As we talked, I started remembering my late father, which made me sad. Dad had been worried about me that day, even as he lay face down in bed.

Nemoto stared at me with sorrow in his eyes as I came next to him. He must have sensed my dampened spirit because he didn't say anything. He must've known my dad had passed away. I'd been absent from school for a week, so there was no way our homeroom teacher hadn't informed the class.

Unable to bear the awkward silence, I spoke again. "So, um…my dad died."

My gaze downcast, I tried to search for what to say, but I had a lump in my throat.

"…I found this hill two or so days ago," Nemoto said. He took his eyes off me. "From here, you can get an unbroken view of the streets of Odawara. See for yourself, Higuchi," he urged, his arms akimbo.

I looked to where he was pointing. Straining my eyes, I could make out the keep of Odawara Castle. Beyond that stretched the bright-green waters of Sagami Bay. That was the first time I'd seen the town where I was born and raised quite like that.

"Listen, Higuchi. I've never lost a parent, so I can't say I understand what you're going through right now. And even if I did, I still wouldn't be able to say that I know what you're going through for sure. I think telling people you get how they feel is super irresponsible. Everybody's operating under different circumstances in life, after all."

He never took his eyes off me.

"But you know what I think?" he continued briskly. "Your father's not around anymore, but you're still around. And you've got a part of him inside you. Meaning, when you're feeling good, he is, too. I'm sure of it. I think your happiness is the basis of *his* happiness. If you ask me, that's what family bonds are all about. Which is why you oughtta focus on doing what you find fun. You should always be smiling."

Those heartfelt words resonated powerfully in my soul.

Ever since I lost my father, one question had plagued me: Had Dad's life been a happy one?

Cursed with a failing heart, he'd been sick for a long time. For the past few years, he'd mostly been bedridden at home. I honestly figured that nothing good had happened to him in his less than fifty years on this Earth. And the thought of how absurdly pitiable his life had been made my chest seize up.

But Nemoto told me that children carried pieces of their parents. Thinking about it that way, there was still more to my father's life after all.

He took out the Snoopy thermos from his school bag. When I accepted the cup he offered me, the tears I'd been desperately holding back started overflowing. Then I heard plodding footsteps from the hill road. I turned to find Shiro winding around my legs.

"Shiro…"

I bent at the knees and patted her head, and she licked the tears that were rolling down my cheeks. She was making a whining noise and wagging her tail contentedly.

"While you were gone from school, she really took to me," said Nemoto. "All right, Shiro, time for snackies!"

He pulled out some beef jerky, and Shiro jumped up to his hand.

"Good girl!" He patted her head, smoothing down the fur.

A black dog appeared from farther down the slope. It strode jauntily across the lawn and started hanging around Shiro.

"Hold on—is he your boyfriend, Shiro?" said Nemoto. "Damn, you're a smooth operator, aren't ya, girl?"

I took a sip of my barley tea and looked up. A bright-blue patch of sky was peeking out from a break in the thick cloud cover.

Starting the next day, we'd take Shiro on forest walks. Nemoto gave Shiro a new collar, a pale-blue one. When we attached a leash to it, we could let Shiro walk wherever she wanted. And it became routine for us to head for that hill after we were done walking her.

At some point, Nemoto started bringing along a camcorder.

"C'mon, Higuchi, gimme a bigger smile than that."

Whenever he asked, I always served him up a smile and a peace sign, the standard photo pose. By that point, lying on our backs atop the hill's soft grass with Shiro nestled between us was our daily ritual.

"I'm usually shy around strangers," he once told me as we partook in this ritual, "but not around you. Wonder why."

Same here, I realized, my heart soaring. *Same here.*

It was then that it dawned on me: I *like* liked him. I liked him as more than just a friend. He had become an irreplaceable presence in my life.

Yet in July of that year, my mother said something that rocked my world. After the end-of-term ceremony at school, we'd be moving to Okayama Prefecture, where my maternal grandmother lived.

My mind went blank. I wouldn't be able to see Shiro anymore. And of course, I wouldn't be able to see Nemoto, either.

I couldn't bring myself to tell him. I hadn't confessed my feelings for him yet, either. Time simply passed by, without any progress on either front. The day before the ceremony, my homeroom teacher announced to the class that I was transferring to another school. None of my classmates looked especially sad, save for one.

I called out to him in class.

"Nemoto…"

His expression stiffened. He didn't respond. Afterward, I tried talking to him whenever I had spare time, but he'd scurry away whenever our eyes met.

On the day of the ceremony, I headed to the forest after it was over. It may have been the last day I'd ever see him, but I was planning to confess to him nonetheless. I couldn't part ways with Nemoto without telling him about how I'd grown feelings for him.

But he wasn't there. Shiro came out to see me, but no matter where I looked, I couldn't find Nemoto. He wasn't by the lake, he wasn't at the hut, and he wasn't at the hill.

Right before heading home, I hugged Shiro tight. *Please take care of yourself, Shiro. And you too, Nemoto.*

I wiped the tears from the corners of my eyes and put behind me this forest, which was so full of memories.

A bonze was reciting sutras in the living room adjoining the entryway. A compact and cozy altar had been installed, with elegant garlands on either side. The funeral attendees rose from their floor cushions and burned incense in turn. Nemoto lay between the altar and incense burner, his coffin dominating the space. My father-in-law, who was next to me, noticed how noisy it had suddenly gotten outside and left his seat.

"Please go away!" he shouted from the yard.

My father-in-law wasn't one to yell like that. He was normally a calm man. The noise was probably the media.

After Nemoto breathed his last in the hospital, his body had been sent to the police for an autopsy. All throughout the two days following the accident, the media had dogged us everywhere we went: *"How are you, a bereaved family member, feeling right now?" "It seems Mr. Nemoto was still alive when he was taken to the hospital. Would you be so kind as to tell us more about what exactly caused his death?"* I wondered how much hurt those cold-blooded questions had inflicted upon the hearts of the other victims' loved ones.

The wake soon ended, the mourners bowing their heads respectfully as they exited the house.

The living room was empty apart from us three now, and my father-in-law sat down beside me. "You okay, Tomo?"

"I'm okay. What about you? Are *you* okay?"

He summoned a smile to reassure me. As the deceased's father, this must have been so tough—he was the chief mourner. He'd handled all the negotiations with the funeral company and talked to the police. I'd offered to help him, but he didn't let me do any of it. He was already over sixty years old, yet ever since the derailment, I'd never heard him say a word about being tired or in pain. Not once.

My mother-in-law came next to me with a tray. "Have yourself an apple, Tomo. I peeled you some."

When Nemoto and I got engaged, my mother-in-law was the happiest of anyone. *"I couldn't have asked for a better daughter-in-law,"* she'd told me once. *"You can even think of me as your actual mother, Tomo, darling!"*

After both my parents died, I was bereft of any family. Nemoto's parents then stepped in to fill that void with more than enough love and affection of their own.

"Oh," I said. "I almost forgot. I've gotta call the wedding venue to cancel."

That was the one thing I couldn't have my in-laws do for me. The wedding was in three months, and the invitations had already been sent out.

My fingertips trembled violently as I tried to tap my phone's screen. Ever since the end of last year when Nemoto proposed to me, I'd been on cloud nine. I couldn't even count the number of times I dreamed of the moment I'd be standing next to him wearing a pure-white dress. And now it had come time to terminate that dream by my own hand.

"Tomo..." My father-in-law squeezed my left hand. "Thank you for falling in love with our Shin'ichirou."

My nose started twitching. I'd thought the well was dry, but there my tears went again. My father-in-law, who'd been trying to hold strong ever since the accident, was shaking, shoulders shuddering. He was biting his lip to keep from crying, but now tears were trickling from his utterly bloodshot eyes.

Kuro emerged from the entryway, yapping. Soon, he was licking the tears streaming down my cheeks. Surrounded by Kuro and my in-laws, I reminisced about the days I started dating Nemoto.

I'd transferred to a high school in Okayama, and after graduating, I became a certified caregiver working at a facility in Okayama City. After I turned thirty, my mother suddenly died. And what a cruel twist of fate that she should die of acute heart failure, same as my father. Even after losing her husband, my mother had still worked nonstop. Maybe she'd broken down from overwork.

My maternal grandmother had passed away by that point as well. Despondent, I decided to return to my hometown of Odawara. I had contacts within the local community, thanks to my part-time job at the old-age home where I worked during my first year of high school. An old acquaintance hooked me up at a nursing facility specializing in elder care.

It happened during the last days of December that year. I dropped by a cheap eatery that had caught my eye on my way home from work.

"I'll have a large *katsudon*. And give me some curry udon, too, thanks."

I gulped down the water in my chipped glass and breathed out audibly through my nose. More than six months had passed since my mother died, and the sense of loss was as fresh as ever. I'd put on a lot of weight; I was well over sixty kilos despite being less than a hundred and sixty centimeters tall. Not only that, but I was also single at an age where it wouldn't be weird to be married with kids. But it was taking all I had to go on living. I couldn't spare a single thought for the future.

"Here you are, ma'am."

The gray-haired lady placed my food on the table. She was dragging her right foot, and there was a foldable wheelchair by the register, so I figured she had a bum leg. She reminded me of my father. Despite how bedridden and ill he'd been, he was always thinking of me. Whenever I'd leave for school, he'd come to the front door using his walking stick and see me off. I was getting emotional.

A man wearing a navy-blue knapsack who was sitting over in the back got to his feet and carried his curry-rice tray to the counter.

"Thanks for the meal. Delicious as always." He picked up one of the dish towels hanging on the rack and wiped his table clean.

"I hate to impose on you like that," said the lady.

"Oh, no, it's nothing," he replied.

I saw his face as he made for the exit, and my chopsticks froze. I recognized that healthy tan and those big, childlike eyes.

"Is that you, Nemoto?"

Grains of rice spilled out of my mouth, but I couldn't have cared less.

"…Higuchi?" he said, his voice going funny and eyes widening like saucers.

We stared at each other until the tears came welling up. He looked exactly the same as I remembered him back in the day. And funnily enough, we'd first met at an eatery not unlike this one. My heart swelled when I remembered what he'd done to rescue me that day.

Due partly to how emotionally unstable I'd been, the tears wouldn't stop.

"Something happen, Higuchi? You okay?"

"Sorry, sorry… I was just thinking you haven't changed at all, Nemoto."

He zipped open his backpack and fetched a handkerchief. He'd opened the side pocket wide enough that I could see the Snoopy thermos there. The very same one he'd used all the time back in high school.

"Huh. I have no idea why I'm crying so much," I said. "It just makes me so happy to see that you haven't changed a bit."

We'd barely even talked yet, but an intense sense of security blanketed my heart. The sparkling memories popping up into view were painting my monochrome world with renewed color.

"…Am I the same as you remember me?" I asked him, trying to think of something cheerier to talk about.

He smiled faintly. "Don't get mad at me, okay, Higuchi? Promise you won't get mad. Because to be honest, I think you gained a little weight."

Then he grinned impishly, scratching his temple with his fingers. His smile was contagious. *When was the last time I smiled this peacefully?* I found myself musing as I wiped my cheeks using the handkerchief he gave me.

Three days later, he and I were together again at that restaurant.

"I've gotta say, you really haven't changed in all this time, Nemoto. You look the same, and you have the same vibe."

"I guess? The people at work keep yelling at me that I'm too much of a kid at heart and that I get too pigheaded."

Before we went our separate ways the day we ran into each other, we'd exchanged contact information. I messaged him, and we decided to grab some dinner. Since our houses weren't far from that restaurant, we settled on the same place as before.

"What do you do for work, Nemoto?"

I sank my teeth into the cutlet at the center of my *katsudon*. I wouldn't normally gobble up my food quite so heartily in front of a guy; I'd purse my lips and eat in a more ladylike fashion, but with him, I didn't feel like I had to hold back.

"I'm working at a pet store near Minami-Kamakura Station," he replied. "You know how I love animals."

Apparently, he'd picked up a certification as a dog trainer right out of high school. *How very like him*, I thought.

"By the way, what happened to Shiro?"

That question had weighed on my mind for fifteen years.

He quietly cleared his throat and deepened his voice. "No need to worry there. My family took her in. Unfortunately, she died three years ago, but I like to think she led a happy life thanks to me."

A pause. "I see."

That was sad news, but it'd been none other than Nemoto who adopted her. She must have loved her life with him.

"There's loads I wanna tell ya about Shiro, so I'll give ya the lowdown one of these days."

I smiled giddily and scarfed down the rest of my meal.

I peppered Nemoto with a whole host of questions about his life, although there was one question I couldn't quite bring myself to ask. I figured I'd extrapolate what I wanted to know in the course of our chat, but although he wasn't wearing a wedding ring, I still wasn't entirely sure. After all, even if he wasn't married, he could nonetheless be going steady with somebody. But now it was time to just straight up ask him.

Having finished eating, he put down his chopsticks, and silence fell between us. I took a deep breath—quietly enough to escape his notice—and stared up at him.

"So, uh…"

"So, uh…," he said at the same time. "You go first," he continued.

I could tell by his awkward expression what he wanted to say, and that put some wind in my sails. "No, *you* go first. Be a man."

"…Uhhh, so… Higuchi, I just wanted to ask: Are you, er, sweet on anybody?"

He was blushing like a little boy. And what a cute, old-fashioned way to put that question. It was so adorable that the tension suddenly melted away.

"Nope, no boyfriend here."

My pride wouldn't let me tell him I'd *never* had a boyfriend.

"Never had one, either—a sweetheart, that is," he replied.

What do you mean, "either"?

But I was happy things were going where I wanted, so I wasn't going to point out the presumptuousness of that remark.

He was clearly feeling shy; he didn't say anything further. He just kept bringing his glass to his lips out of nervousness. Not exactly ideal, but in the end, my unvarnished feelings for him made me speak up.

"If you're interested—"

"If you're interested—"

It happened again.

I giggled, and so did he. Neither of us said anything else. We just kept chuckling. And that was how we started dating.

"Mother, could you taste the curry for me?"

I handed her a small dish with the roux in it, and after taking a sip, she flashed me the okay sign. It was my late mom who'd taught me this curry recipe.

"Let me taste-test, too," said my father-in-law, who emerged from the warm *kotatsu*. He sipped some from a china spoon and gave me a thumbs-up, all smiles.

About two months after we began dating, I started dropping by Nemoto's house. I'd lost my parents, and his parents treated me warmly. His dad was retired, so he spent his days at home. We'd often enjoy dinner together, the four of us.

"Come have a taste, too, Nemoto."

Nemoto was reading a book at the *kotatsu*.

"My goodness, you two," said my mother-in-law, frowning, "you're *dating*. When are you gonna call each other by your first names?"

"It's fine, Mom. This works for us."

We were both shy, so neither of us would ever be able address the other by their first name. But that was so *us* that it felt good. That was how we'd addressed each other back in the day, too, so we decided to keep it this way. I called him "Nemoto," and he called me "Higuchi."

"Damn, that's good!" he exclaimed. "You gotta make me some curry for my birthday next month."

I grinned with satisfaction.

The dog outside started barking, perhaps out of envy—the curry smelled pretty good. This was Kuro, a big male dog the family owned. Nemoto must have trained him well, because he took super kindly to people.

"C'mon in, Kuro."

Nemoto opened the front door, and Kuro rushed into the dining room. He shook out his black coat of fur and then stood up on his hind legs and leaped at me: *Food! Give me food!*

In that moment, I found myself reflecting on how stupidly happy I was. I was wrapped in so much warmth, I felt as though I could reach out and actually *touch* it. I couldn't help but hope that this bliss would last forever and ever.

Outside the windows, the harsh December winds were blowing. A person in a trench coat had their shoulders hunched against the biting breeze.

"Here you are, madame. *Le poisson du jour.*"

A pointlessly huge plate was placed in front of me.

"Apparently, *poisson* means *fish*," I told Nemoto under my breath, seeing how nervous he was about not knowing the proper way to eat it. (I was no smarty-pants; I'd just looked it up on my phone.)

That day, we were celebrating my thirty-second birthday. We decided to eat out for the occasion, but he wanted to surprise me, so he didn't tell me where he was taking me beforehand. We met up at Minami-Kamakura Station after work, and he walked me over to this French restaurant. While there was no dress code, we were fish out of water compared with the other patrons, who all had an elegant and refined air to them. Neither he nor I had ever been to a restaurant this high-end before, and naturally, we didn't know the first thing about the expected table manners.

A man in a black tuxedo bent at the waist to face us. "Wine is included in your course. What would you like?"

Neither of us could tolerate much alcohol. The words *If I don't drink it, could we get that much of our money back?* nearly made it out of my mouth before I banished the thought.

"Okay, I'll have a little red wine in a cup," I said, putting on airs.

"A little in a glass, then," the man replied, correcting me.

A glass, not a cup. Part of it was just my own paranoia, but I felt like he was making fun of me, and I couldn't stand it.

Nemoto dropped his knife to the floor, and he made to pick it up.

A nearby employee stopped him with a hand. "Allow *me*, sir."

Those words came out sounding barbed, as if to say, *You dopes don't know what you're doing, do you?*

I felt so *watched* after that. Like my every action was being scrutinized. It was unsettling; I couldn't get myself to calm down.

"All right, Higuchi, let's wish ya happy birthday one more time. Cheers!"

We'd gone back to Odawara and were now clinking cups of orange juice at the same old food joint as always.

"I'm real sorry about all that, Higuchi," he said, sitting across from me. "Forgive me for ruining your birthday."

"It's okay, Nemoto. Though, it pretty much confirmed my feelings—I shouldn't be doing stuff that isn't me."

I put my cup to my lips, knitting my brows.

"Happy birthday, Tomoko, dear. This one's on the house."

The restaurant lady served me a large plate of steamed vegetables. I was a familiar face at this point.

"Sorry to keep ya waiting, Higuchi, but here. Your present."

Nemoto handed me a large paper bag. I took out the present and unwrapped it to find a black tote bag inside. Not too long ago, he'd come with me to visit my parents' graves. The shoulder strap of my bag came off, so we hit up a department store, but all the bags we looked at had been prohibitively expensive.

"You went and bought me a replacement for my bag. That must've cost you!"

"Don't mention it. And here, I got ya some sneakers, too." He took out a second paper bag. "The shoes you're always wearing look pretty beat-up. And look, I got ya a memory foam cushion. You keep mentioning your back hurts. Plus, there's this guy here…"

With that, he placed a smallish, unwrapped, royal-blue case on the table. Oblivious, I slowly opened it until I saw enthroned in the lustrous fabric—a ring sporting a big shiny diamond.

"Higuchi."

I was speechless.

"Marry me?"

A straight, point-blank proposal. He hadn't been shy about it like when he'd sort of asked me out.

I was taken aback by the suddenness of it all. Before any wave of happiness, what struck me first was a mounting sense of amusement. I was in the one universe where a guy would propose at a greasy spoon like this place. But I didn't hate that unaffected part of him. In fact, I actively liked it. Whether it came to birthdays or to proposals, this kind of eatery fit us the best.

Come to think of it, it's been nearly a year since we reunited at this place. All the stuff that had happened in that time streamed into my brain in chronological order.

"…Yes."

I pulled my head back and straightened up in embarrassment. Trying to hide my bashfulness, I reached for some of my stir-fried vegetables with my chopsticks, but my vision had gotten blurrier, and I was having trouble grabbing any. Eventually, I managed to pick up some white bean sprouts; they were tasty, with a nice crunch to them.

Ever since he proposed to me, I'd been wrapped in a robe of pure elation. Whenever I was near him, I felt like I was floating on a cloud.

One early spring day in Kamakura, when the storm winds were signaling winter's end, I was working my nursing-home job. Nemoto's birthday was coming up the following week. *Might as well take the opportunity to make him a different recipe than usual*, I thought as I tended to the needs of one of our elderly clients.

"You're going wedding-dress shopping soon?" asked my boss, who patted me on the shoulder as we crossed paths in the hallway leading to the cafeteria. "Color this old maid jealous!"

Her name was Ms. Yamada, and ever since I got engaged, she'd been teasing me at every opportunity. The wedding ceremony was going to be held on June 3 at a hotel in Kamakura. Nemoto and I had gone there to check out a seaside chapel, and that was when we decided.

I had yet to put on my ring. I was a caretaker—there was no way I could come to work wearing a diamond ring. I was planning to slip it on for the first time on the day I'd choose my wedding dress.

"Ms. Higuchi," Ms. Yamada whispered in my ear, "it looks as though Mr. Ujiki's arrived." She dashed to the entrance.

Mr. Ujiki was in the early stages of dementia, although his absentmindedness wasn't so bad that he couldn't manage on his own. But he'd lost his granddaughter about two weeks prior and hadn't come to the facility for any nursing care since. He was looking positively gaunt: pale in the face and eyes so sunken, it looked like he'd taken a punch or two.

Ms. Yamada led the way, taking Mr. Ujiki to the staff lounge down the hall. Me and the other employees in the lounge exchanged a look, and they nodded in understanding before exiting. Mr. Ujiki sat cross-legged on the tatami mat that was there for naps.

"Would you like something to drink, Mr. Ujiki?" I asked him.

I craned my head closer, but no response. *As a caretaker, what should I say during times like these?*

He pulled out a small pink spiral seashell from his jacket pocket, staring at it fondly.

"What a pretty shell," I said, smiling at him.

"It's a memento of my late granddaughter," he said, forcing the words from his lips. "When she was in elementary school, she said she wanted to go collect seashells, so we went to Enoshima together. She was such a sweet kid that she gave me one of the two pink conch shells she'd found. 'One for me, one for you. It's a pair!' Why'd a kid as sweet as her have to…?"

He hung his head, his eyes tearing up. I didn't know what to say. *Maybe during times like these, I should just let them grieve alone.*

"I'll come back later, Mr. Ujiki," I said quietly before exiting the lounge.

The lobby was noisier. On the LCD screen, a train was on its side, and the old folks who'd gathered around were glued to the TV.

"Ms. Higuchi!" Ms. Yamada, who'd returned to the office, came around the corner of the hallway, her slippers pitter-pattering all the while. "Looks like a Mrs. Nemoto's on the phone for you."

Guess it's Nemoto's mom. It was rare for her to call me at work, so that was weird. I shuffled over to the office and picked up the phone at the desk.

"Hello?"

"Hey, Tomo, honey, sorry to call you at work."

"What's wrong, Mother?"

"Try to take what I'm about to say calmly. The train Shin'ichirou was on just derailed."

"What?"

"Shin'ichirou's train just derailed!"

"Is…is Nemoto okay? Is he all right—?"

"Just come straight to Minami-Kamakura General Hospital. Bye."

When I hung up the phone, I could feel my heartbeat gradually quickening. As the icy grip of anxiety clung to my whole body, I got into a taxi at the urging of one of my coworkers. Soon, I'd come face-to-face with his lifeless body at the hospital.

That was the moment when the happiness that had wrapped me up was replaced by the coldest of cloaks.

Nemoto's funeral ended before I could even process how I felt.

Two weeks after the derailment, his parents and I were at a large hotel in Kamakura. A briefing session for victims held by Touhin, the company that owned the train, was starting just past noon. In a spacious room normally used as a banquet hall, the ranks of the Touhin management team were seated in a neat little row across from the rest of us in our folding chairs.

"As for the indemnities," the corporation's elderly president, who was seated in the center, announced in a businesslike tone, "those will be handled in an orderly fashion once the accident-investigation committee has reached a conclusion."

The way he was talking, it sounded like he was saying, *As long as we pay you off, we're good as gold*, which sparked our irritation.

"This ain't a question o' money!" somebody shouted.

The president looked unfazed. "In any case, it appears as though it was the conductor who caused the incident," he replied. One could read into that statement that Touhin was positioning themselves as victims, too.

Sixty-eight of the hundred and twenty-seven passengers had died. And with over forty seriously injured and some still unresponsive, the death toll was only going to get higher. The numbers attested to what an unprecedented disaster this was, and yet here they were, giving us more lame excuses than expressions of remorse. We were annoyed from the very start.

Touhin came right out the gate chalking it up to the excessive speeds the conductor had reached. However, when the victims attending the briefing session asked for an explanation as to what led up to that, Touhin wasn't exactly forthcoming. They told us things like "Since the conductor died as well, we don't know the details at this stage" and "We're waiting for the accident-investigation committee's conclusion."

"This is just my personal opinion, but the fact that there were no casualties other than the passengers is, I think, a silver lining," said the president without any ill will.

That was the straw that broke the camel's back.

"You've got to be joking…" My hands balled into fists. "You've *got* to be joking!"

Driven by an impulse I couldn't name, I shot to my feet.

"There *is* no silver lining when an accident claims people's lives! Do you people even understand what you've done?" I said, fire in my voice. "The derailment took my beloved fiancé away from me. And his life isn't the only thing you people stole. You stole his future. His isn't the only future that's been stolen, either: *My* future's now one without him in it. Do you even realize that you've robbed the victims' loved ones of their futures? Don't just sit there! Answer me, why don't you?!"

I left my chair, shaking off the people trying to stop me as I walked up to the rows of suited men.

"Answer me!" I cried. "Go on, say something! Give us your answer!"

My father-in-law grabbed my arm from behind, pulling me close and hugging me tight. He was trembling a little, and his upper body felt bizarrely sweaty. Tears flooded my eyes even more when I realized how much thinner he'd gotten since the accident.

"Tomoko, honey, I gave you a generous portion for your *katsudon*."

The lady at my usual greasy spoon gently placed a tray in front of me. "Chin up," she said, putting a hand on my shoulder.

I flashed her a strained smile.

Over the two months following the derailment, I'd been holed up at home. Although I was finally able to return to my job at the end of April, I still couldn't put down my mood-stabilizing meds, not even at work. It took little for me to suffer another bout of depression and suddenly hate life again.

I had no appetite for food whatsoever. I heaved a sigh of fatigue and weakly reached out for a pair of disposable chopsticks.

"Have you heard the rumors about the ghost at Nishi-Yuigahama Station?"

I overheard an odd conversation from the next table down. Two women were talking after having finished their meals.

"No, what rumors?"

"You know that train on the Kamakura Line that derailed a little while ago? Recently, they say it appears late at night where the accident happened—Nishi-Yuigahama Station."

"'It'?"

"The ghost. Somebody I know through work lost family in the accident, and they saw this ghost lady in Nishi-Yuigahama in the dead of night."

"No freaking way."

"It's not just them, either. There are folks who saw a translucent train go down the Kamakura Line in the middle of the night—and some people even *boarded* that train. It's been the talk of the town in my neighborhood."

"Wonder if it's got anything to do with Kamakura Ikitama Shrine?"

"It might. They did say the train hit the torii of Ikitama Shrine when it derailed. And word has it that shrine's been freaky for ages."

My chopsticks froze before I could grab the bit of cutlet in my *katsudon*. Kamakura Ikitama Shrine—a small shrine in Minami-Kamakura. According to legend, departed souls remained among the living there. Reports of ghost sightings were rampant; I'd heard such stories who knows how many times when I was a kid. And in my current headspace, I couldn't ignore the idea. If I could see Nemoto again…

Hoping against hope, I decided to visit Nishi-Yuigahama Station to see for myself.

"Ma'am, it's midnight; we'll be closing shop now."

I drank the rest of my hot chocolate and exited the café. A little distance ahead, amid the residential area, lay the station platform. Beyond the residences south of the station stretched Yuigahama Beach; listen closely, and you could hear the waves from here, albeit faintly. Both inbound and outbound service had been suspended for the Kamakura Line even though the scene of the accident had already been inspected. I'd arrived by taxi from Odawara.

In the tense silence, I sat on the bench near the railroad crossing. I looked long and hard at the entire lengthy platform, but I saw no ghost lady. Was it just a silly rumor?

If nothing happens by one AM, *I'm heading home.*

That very moment, a black train sped down the tracks from the previous station, Chigasaki Kaigan. Translucent as if blending into the darkness, it seemed to get bigger as it neared Nishi-Yuigahama Station. I could scarcely believe my eyes; there was a significant number of people on board.

I crossed the still-open ticket gate, heart racing. When I stepped onto the empty platform, the train screeched to a halt.

"You see this train?" came a voice. "Only folks with strong feelings about the accident can."

A girl slowly approached from the other end of the platform.

"They're also the only ones who can hear the train. Looks like you're one of 'em."

She stopped in front of me, her narrow eyes falling on me. She was tall, so the pose she struck with her arms folded was a little intimidating.

My expression was doubtful. "Are you...a ghost?"

"Sure am," she replied, smoothing back her bangs.

"You got a name or anything?"

"My name's Yukiho. As you can see, I'm a high school kid."

She was wearing what looked like a school uniform with a light-purple ribbon tied around her white long-sleeve blouse's collar. Her short skirt was the same color as the ribbon. Her legs were slender and well proportioned, and her prettiness made me feel less confused and afraid.

I had questions, but I didn't know where to start. Then the train slowly started moving again.

Yukiho looked in the direction it was traveling and muttered, "A little while after the train passes through Nishi-Yuigahama, it vanishes."

A few minutes after she said that, there was a thunderous crash far off in the distance.

"...What do you mean by that?" I asked, leaning in closer to Yukiho. She trained her eyes on me again.

"I hate beating around the bush, so I'll make it simple: The train that just passed by is the very same train that derailed from the Kamakura Line on March fifth of this year. And you can board it if you like."

"Huh?"

"You can go and see the people who rode the train on that day."

I paused. "I can see somebody who died?"

"Yep. But there's four rules people who board need to keep in mind."

Then she laid them out:

- You may board the train only from the station where the doomed rider first boarded.
- You mustn't tell the doomed rider that they are soon to die.
- You must get off the train at or before passing Nishi-Yuigahama Station. Otherwise, you, too, shall die in the accident.
- Meeting the doomed rider will not change their fate. No matter what you do, those who died in the accident will not come back to life. If you attempt to get people off the train before it derails, you will be returned to the present day.

I had more than a few questions, but the rule that particularly caught my attention was the last one. Meeting Nemoto wouldn't change my reality. No matter what I did, the dead would stay dead.

"If you can abide by those four rules, head to the station where the victim boarded. You can go as soon as late tomorrow night. That train'll pull into your station." Yukiho refolded her arms before giving a little wave good-bye. "See you."

She disappeared. The phantasmal way she vanished lent credence to everything she'd told me, and I had no misgivings. Reality didn't *have* to change. He didn't have to come back to life for me to want to see him again.

By one AM the next day, I went to Odawarajou-mae Station, where Nemoto had boarded the doomed train. It was the closest station to us, one that I used all the time, so I knew where to go.

There was no sign of anyone else around the station; I stepped through the ticket gate and onto the platform.

It happened just as I was about to take one of the pills prescribed by my doctor to calm my nerves. My surroundings suddenly turned bright, and before I knew it, a middle-aged woman was standing next to me. On the platform across from me, there were a great many office workers waiting for the outbound train. The watch on my left wrist read 10:44 AM. I'd been transported to that platform on the morning of the derailment. The rhythmic rumbling of the train reverberated from down the tracks.

"Now arriving at Odawarajou-mae," came the even-tempered announcement. *"This is Odawarajou-mae Station."*

The black train I saw the night prior stopped at the platform, the sound of its brakes trailing. Its doors opened with a *pshhh*. I was frozen in mute amazement at this series of incredible events when a small man wearing a navy-blue backpack passed through the ticket gate.

"Nemoto…," I said.

I hid my face with my bag so that he wouldn't notice me. He boarded the second car of the six-car train. I slipped into his car by way of the next door over, and then the train's wheels slowly started turning again.

The train looked translucent on the outside, but the inside was no different from any ordinary train. Both the bench seating along one side and the box seats that faced each other were the same colors as usual.

Still, it seemed there were fewer people on board than the actual media-reported number of passengers at the time of the accident. Sure, more people got on at stations after this one, but there were fewer than twenty people here in Car Two. Maybe the survivors weren't on this ghost train?

Nemoto was in a box seat by the gangway between the cars.

"Next stop, Maekawa. Maekawa Station."

There was no time to get sentimental. Upon hearing the announcement, I put the strategy I'd come up with beforehand into action. The moment the doors opened at Maekawa Station, I ran in front of him.

"Nemoto, we're getting off!"

"Higuchi…," he said, surprised.

I forced him to his feet and dragged him out the door.

But as soon as we got off the train and the doors closed behind us, the sky turned dark, and the ghost train disappeared, Nemoto along with it. I stood there, stunned.

"I'm pretty sure I told you that if you try taking someone off the train, you'd snap back to reality."

Yukiho appeared behind me from out of nowhere.

"You're all the same, you know. So skeptical of the rules I lay out for you. You think maybe if they get off the train, they'll be spared. Well, sorry to break it to you, but there's no chance of that happening."

I had no words in reply.

"I'll say it again," she began huffily, folding her arms in an imposing manner. "You can meet someone who died, but they won't come back to life, and it won't change a thing in real life, either. If that's fine by you, then board this train. Also, the ghost train is fading away a little more every day. I suspect it'll ascend into heaven at some point not far in the future, so don't go thinking you'll get plenty of chances. See you."

Kuro was sprawled out on the floor when he got to his feet and rested his chin on my thigh. Rubbing his head, I washed down another pill. I was in the dining room of Nemoto's house, just me and the dog. I recalled Yukiho's words the night prior:

"You can meet someone who died, but they won't come back to life, and it won't change a thing in real life, either. If that's fine by you, then board this train."

I pondered, using the table to rest my chin in my hands. Now I was starting to think that getting on the train to see him would only make me suffer more. Nothing would change either way. Besides, what would I even talk to him about to begin with? Yukiho's second rule forbade me from telling him he was about to die. If that weren't the case, I could offer Nemoto some parting words, but I had no such option.

"I'm home," my father-in-law announced as he entered. "Today's Sunday, so there was traffic." He then sat down across from me.

"Tomo, you did eat your lunch today, didn't you?" asked my mother-in-law, who took a seat next to her husband.

"I did. It was good."

"I see…," she replied before putting a large paper bag by her feet.

In truth, I'd lacked the appetite to touch the stew she'd made for me. It seemed as though they both saw through my lie. I could tell from their probing eyes.

"Ever since the accident, I've been running around too much to tell you," my father-in-law said, taking off his suit jacket. "But from this point forward, consider yourself our daughter. And as our daughter, you don't gotta worry about a thing. We just want you to lean on us with whatever troubles you might have."

My mother-in-law picked up where he left off, as if she'd been waiting her turn. "And let me add a little something myself: No matter what anybody might say, you'll *always* be my daughter. Apologies to your dearly departed parents, but we're snatching you up. Me and my husband got to talking last night, and… would you care to live with us, Tomo? We're no spring chickens anymore, so you being here would help us out. If we go senile, be a dear and look after us!"

She smiled amiably.

The two had come back from a visit to an attorney's office. I'd offered to come along, but they wouldn't let me (*"We'll take care of all the small stuff regarding the accident"*).

The paper bag she'd put on the floor caught my eye; it had the logo of a pumpkin-pudding store in Tokyo. I'd told my in-laws that I liked that place's pudding in the past. They'd gone all the way to Tokyo to buy me some.

It reminded me of their kindness when I started seeing a shrink and they accompanied me to my first appointment. I'd never forget what my father-in-law told me as I was waiting in the lobby for my evaluation:

"Tomo, your emotional scars are proof you're taking life seriously. People who just glide through life never get hurt. You genuinely loved a fellow human being, and for that reason, your heart's feeling under the weather. Mental illness is rooted in the sufferer's sense of faith and integrity. And I think you can wear that as a badge of pride."

I needed to express my gratitude to these saints I called parents. And to Nemoto as well. He was always the one who cast sunshine on my life. I had to look him in the face one last time and thank him for everything.

But I was in *rough* shape. Would I be able to maintain my composure when I saw him? Yukiho's third rule sprang to mind:

You must get off the train at or before passing Nishi-Yuigahama Station. Otherwise, you, too, shall die in the accident.

I exhaled, expelling the air from deep within me. With so many different thoughts and feelings knocking around in my head, I decided to board that train once again.

* * *

"Now arriving at Odawarajou-mae. This is Odawarajou-mae Station."

The see-through train arrived at the platform, its black doors opening with a *pshhh* of air.

I was seated on the platform bench, and Nemoto hurried past me with his backpack on. I saw him rush through the car's second door, just like last time, and I entered through that same door.

Once again, he took a seat next to the gangway connecting that car to Car Three. Then he put his backpack on the floor by his feet and rested his arm on the window's edge before setting his eyes on the rolling scenery.

I spent a moment gazing at his face from a short distance away. Since it took the train only forty-one minutes to get to Nishi-Yuigahama Station, I didn't have a second to waste. But even so, I kept staring. He was wearing the same expression as he had on all the dates we'd gone on. I'd looked up at his face from the side as we walked hand in hand all the time. I liked how his features still had a cherubic quality to them.

Once I took the seat opposite him, I'd never see his face like this ever again.

"Nemoto," I said after the doors closed.

"Higuchi…"

"I've got some minor business to take care of."

I took the seat opposite him, my gaze downcast. I was so disoriented that I hesitated to look him in the eyes.

I rummaged through the tote bag at my feet and pretended to search for something, just buying time to try to calm myself down a little. I took a deep breath quietly enough so that he didn't notice and slowly raised my head.

The moment his face came into view, everything I'd been planning to say flew away. The face that had haunted my dreams every night over the past two months was so close that I could feel his breath. My mind went blank, and I couldn't summon any words. I checked my watch; it had already been about five minutes since we'd boarded. The thought of having to bid him farewell in a little over half an hour made my vision blur.

I covered my face with both hands. After all this time, I still couldn't come to terms with it, try as I might.

My voice was quavering. "I'm sorry. I'm so sorry…"

Tears surged from deep in my eye sockets like they knew no end. Yet the eyes looking back at me exhibited a quiet grace. He didn't ask what was the matter, just as he never had. Whenever I got upset, he'd wait until I calmed down before asking what was wrong.

He had no way of knowing of my current predicament, but I'd lost around ten kilos since his death. Anybody would be befuddled as to how their fiancée lost that much weight in such a short span of time, but if he felt that way, he didn't show it. He did me the favor of simply looking on watchfully and waiting for me to stop crying.

"I'm sorry, Nemoto. The wedding's right around the corner, so I'm a bit of an emotional wreck right now…"

A plausible explanation. I dug my hand into my bag, using my other hand to decline the handkerchief he tried to lend me and fetching a hand towel to wipe my tears.

The act of crying had allowed me to expel a little of the baggage that had accumulated in my heart.

I scanned the area in search of some topic to lighten the conversation. Then I hit upon something at last: *Oh yeah, Nemoto, it's your birthday*. But I swallowed those words just in time. After all, he'd never see another day.

Nemoto was the one to break the silence. "Gotta say, nice view, huh?" He stretched. "Always loved staring out at the sea from this train."

His expression lit up, and his eyes fell on the scenery outside the window. Beyond the rows of houses lay the blue, blue expanse.

"I've used this train since I was a kid. I like thinking about stuff while watching the waves in the distance. The ocean's so endless, it makes me feel like my own future's boundless, y'know? Just looking at it gives me courage. Love the ocean, man. Love it."

The train stopped at Koiso Station. The doors closed, but not before the coastal breeze brought in the faint sea air.

"Nemoto… Can I ask you a question?" The words rushed out of my mouth, not least because my nerves had subsided with time. "As embarrassing as it is for me to ask this question to your face."

"Lay it on me."

"It's just… I was wondering: What about me did you, uh, fall in love with?"

I'd never been able to bring myself to ask him before. And that was because I had no confidence in myself, my looks included.

He smiled broadly. His reaction, far from bashful, was boastful in a way. "There's a lot to love about ya, but the number one thing for me is how much I enjoy my time with you. I have a great time when we chat, I have a great time when we share a meal, I have a great time when we hang out with Kuro. The time we spend together is always such a treat."

I said nothing.

"Plus, I love how you always order the *katsudon* at the restaurant."

"Wait, what?"

"Your average lady would be too embarrassed to order a bowl of *katsudon*. So I like watching you go to town on some."

"Fine, I see how it is. Well, you hold your chopsticks all wrong. And it never improves no matter how many times I point out the right way," I said, pouting.

Laughing, he scratched his head when I called him out like that. He was teasing me, but I was happy he told me what he really thought. I got the feeling that the way he saw me was very *him*.

"You've always been yourself. Never artificial, never unnatural. And that should never change," he told me.

I paused. "Let me pose a hypothetical. And this is a big *if*, okay?"

Taking advantage of the flow of the conversation, I decided to ask the question I thought to ask in advance. There was some hesitation there; it was a question that required courage. But after taking a deep breath, that was where I steered the discussion.

"If you were to die in the near future, how would you feel if I wanted to die soon afterward, too?"

This ghost train prohibited one from telling a passenger that their life was about to end, but I figured it'd be okay if I phrased it this way. I really needed an answer to that question. That strategy must have worked, as the train didn't vanish on me again.

He remained silent, so I continued, "Don't worry, it's just a hypothetical question. Think of it as a joke, basically. If you died, then could I—?"

"No," he said instantly.

I said nothing.

"No, you're not allowed. I'd never forgive you."

"……"

Those words were a punch to the gut; I flinched hard. It was a complete one-eighty from his gentle gaze up until that point. He was glaring at me. I'd never seen him like this.

"Higuchi," he said softly, his expression relaxing again. "All I ask of you is this."

I stayed silent.

"As long as you're happy, that's all I need. I want you to have fun playing with Kuro and to relish the *katsudon* you chow down on. I just want you to always live life smiling. I want you smiling ten years from now, then twenty years from now. I want you smiling when you're a little old biddy. Always and forever."

"……"

The train pulled into Chigasaki Kaigan Station. This station's platform was so familiar; the door to memory lane swung open.

Around when Nemoto and I started dating, my head had been filled with work-related worries. Once, on a day off, the two of us boarded the train back to Odawara after sharing some dinner in Kamakura. He'd always listen to me talk about my concerns, whether over a meal or on the return train ride.

The next day, my help had been needed at a welfare facility near Chigasaki Kaigan Station. Since I had to get to work early in the morning, I'd booked a hotel near the coast. After arriving at Chigasaki Kaigan Station and waving Nemoto good-bye, I took a seat on a bench on the platform and hung my head. Thinking about work the next day, I couldn't muster the will to go to the hotel.

I was glued to the bench when suddenly, I felt a tap on the shoulder. I looked up to find him there sitting next to me.

"What're you doing here, Nemoto?"

"I realized I can't just leave you all alone."

He'd taken the trouble of getting off at the next stop and turning right back around. He must have seen me hanging my head on the bench after the train had already left the station. Then he proceeded to listen to me talk until the last train of the day was gone.

"...Nemoto, why are you always so nice to me?" I asked as the doomed train started heading for the next stop, Nishi-Yuigahama.

"Isn't it obvious?" A faint smile showed through. "Because you're you."

A pause.

"Because you're *you*, Higuchi."

"........."

It felt like the hands of the clock suddenly froze.

After a little while, my heart swelled.

Just how much does this man care about me? I'm not particularly cute or stylish or sexy, and it's not like I've got a lot of money.

And yet he'd chosen me. He'd loved me and protected me.

Whenever I thought about him, the first thing that sprang to mind was him sitting next to me after I ordered that *kake udon*. He'd enveloped a penniless girl like me with his overwhelming kindness. The world was cold and harsh in so many ways; how many people as considerate as him could possibly be out there?

I could still remember it all like it was yesterday. The way he faced Shiro in the woods in that heavy rain. The way I pulled him up from the flooding lake. In every page in my tome of memories that warmed my heart, he was there. All the radiance and brightness in my life was thanks to him.

In my reverie, the conductor's announcement sounded like it was coming from a long ways away. *"Next stop, Nishi-Yuigahama."*

I retrieved the ring box from my bag. "Nemoto. Today, I'm...I'm gonna..." I psyched myself up and stared at him. "I... So I, uh, brought the ring with me today. Since I never slipped it on in front of you before."

I took the ring out of the case. When I tried to put it on my finger, he swiped the ring from me.

"……"

Then he gently grabbed my left hand. Without either of us saying a word, he slipped it onto my ring finger little by little, the tears in his eyes quietly spilling over like raindrops falling from trees and leaving beautiful streaks running slowly down his cheeks. Before I knew it, our lips were touching. His soft lips filled me with something that words could never describe.

The train began to rapidly decelerate. I swallowed the sob that had built up at the back of my throat and tore my lips off his, getting to my feet and turning away from him before moving to the door. If I saw his face once more time, I wouldn't be able to leave the train.

But I had one more thing to tell him. Words of gratitude.

I needed to give him a proper thank you.

The wheels slowly came to a stop. I steeled my resolve and made to face him again. Yet I caught myself just as I was about to say it.

I couldn't.

To say one last thank-you would be to officially part ways forever.

"Nemoto…"

Since the derailment, I'd cried and wept and bawled my eyes out. And after all those tears, the emotion that remained in my heart… It wasn't a feeling of gratitude.

I couldn't say thank you. I couldn't say farewell.

And that was because…I loved him. Simple as that.

"Nemoto."

The train door opened. I wiped the tears from my eyes, turned around, and summoned all my strength to show him a smile.

"I'll make you curry for your birthday next week."

A long wedding aisle in a glass chapel with the sea at its back, and a dazzling stream of natural light pouring from beyond the large panes.

The day after boarding the ghost train, I dropped by the hotel in Kamakura where I'd planned to hold my wedding. I'd canceled the ceremony two
months prior, but I still felt the urge to see the venue one last time.

"Ms. Higuchi?"

A young woman called out to me in the passageway connecting the chapel
to the main building. She was the planner who'd been in charge of my
wedding.

"I'm so sorry for your loss, ma'am." She bowed so deeply that *I* felt humbled. "As a wedding planner and as a woman, it breaks my heart that we
couldn't hold the ceremony for you and Mr. Nemoto."

"Thank you, but really, I should apologize to you for the inconvenience."

Since I first visited the hotel, she'd given us her counsel so warmly. Though
the ceremony was no more, I was still extremely grateful.

She couldn't totally hide that distressed look on her face.

"Ms. Higuchi, there's something I've been wrestling with talking to you
about, but… Mr. Nemoto—he asked me to edit a video to be shown at the
reception. He was planning for it to be a surprise, so he told me to keep it a
secret from you. And because of my duty to keep things confidential, I
couldn't tell you without some hand-wringing, even after that terrible accident… The video is ready, but…"

I could tell from the pregnant pause that she was waiting for me to make
the request.

"Please show it to me," I urged.

"Yes, ma'am, understood," she said, bowing her head.

With her help, I decided to watch the video at the ceremony hall, where I
was supposed to have taken it in alongside Nemoto. The planner led me inside
the vast chamber, which was probably capable of accommodating around a
hundred and fifty people. The tables weren't laid out, but there were hotel
workers in the corner preparing flowers and place cards, probably to be used
for a reception the next day.

"Here, ma'am, please take a seat."

A male employee brought a round table to the center of the hall. I thanked him and sat down. Then the planner brewed me some herbal tea right there at the table.

"Now then, allow us to start the video."

At her signal, the lights turned dim, and a screen descended from the other end of the hall.

FOR HIGUCHI

That handwritten title text appeared in the center of a pure-white screen before it was replaced by a panoramic view of a vast forest. A white dog was running around various locales—the sloped trail, the side of the lake, and that hill…

This was footage of Shiro that Nemoto had taken when we were in our freshman year of high school. And there I was. My high school freshman self, holding Shiro's leash, taking her for a walk. Cut to me squatting down with my back to the lake, looking all embarrassed as Shiro was licking my mouth. (She'd stolen my first kiss!)

Cut to me lying on the grass on the hill alongside Shiro, hands behind my head.

"C'mon, Higuchi, gimme a bigger smile than that." My younger self made a peace sign and smiled contentedly.

I was smiling in all these shots. I looked like I was having fun. I looked happy. No—I *was* happy.

My eyes were glued to the screen while the tightly edited shots rolled by. As the video wore on, my dry and desiccated heart sprang back to life like it had reached an oasis. The forest footage gave way to footage of his house, in the garden where Nemoto was throwing a Frisbee to Shiro.

"Where are you throwing it, Shin'ichirou?" came my mother-in-law's voice; she was manning the camera.

Suddenly, a little black dog appeared at Nemoto's feet. *"You wanna play Frisbee, too?"* he asked, and the black dog started wagging its tail happily.

"Kuro is Shiro's pup," came Nemoto's narration over the zoomed-in puppy.

My breath caught in my throat.

"I kept it from you this whole time in order to surprise you."

I remembered there'd been a black dog in that forest. A dog that'd been good friends with Shiro. They'd often walked together, almost like a couple. Kuro, the dog the Nemoto family was keeping now, was Shiro's puppy.

Nemoto continued speaking, this time over footage of Shiro and Kuro playing together.

"I'm sorry I gave you the cold shoulder after I found out you were transferring to Okayama. I just couldn't accept losing you. I couldn't meet face-to-face and say good-bye. I couldn't bring myself to go to the woods on your last day in town. Looking back, I was being childish. I'm truly sorry. Shiro had taken a liking to you and me, but I hadn't intended to take her in. It was only after you left that I decided to keep Shiro as a real pet. That's because I thought that if my family adopted Shiro right away, I'd no longer see you in that forest. I've had feelings for you ever since we met there. The reason I never left my hometown after graduating high school is because I figured if I stayed, there was a chance I could see you again."

Finally, as the video was nearing its end, he imparted the following words:

"Once the reception's over, let's go and visit those woods together."

I stepped through the murky drainage gutter in my sneakers. *Splash, splash, splash.* I remembered the tactile sensation of the tangle of waterweeds, and the apartments on each side were also the same as way back then.

"Don't rush off like that, Kuro!"

Kuro was looking back at me in front of the bridge spanning the irrigation canal, his enthusiastic tail-wagging encouraging me to come quick.

Three days after that video, I was taking Kuro to those woods.

Surprisingly, the forest hadn't changed in the least. The wooden hut near the lake was still there, the same as ever. As if guided by Kuro, I set foot on the hill with the great view, the shiny tree stump-chair, and the lush green grass.

"Nothing's changed here, either, huh?"

I saw Kuro lie down on the grass, and I stretched out spread-eagle next to him. As I looked up at the sky, what Nemoto said on this hill after my father passed away ran through my head:

"Your father's not around anymore, but you're still around. And you've got a

part of him inside you. Meaning, when you're feeling good, he is, too. I'm sure of it. I think your happiness is the basis of his happiness. If you ask me, that's what family bonds are all about."

Kuro started running around the hill with a gleeful expression.

Kuro is Shiro's successor, I thought. *And when Kuro's happy, so is the late Shiro. And when the baby inside me is happy, Nemoto will be happy, too. I'm sure of it.*

I went to the doctor the other day because I was feeling ill—and found out I was pregnant.

To make our unborn child happy was to make Nemoto happy. Upon reflection, I realized he'd always been by my side during every crisis in my life. When I was in high school and my father passed away, he'd been there. After my mother passed away and I was depressed, he'd been there. And now that he'd passed away and I was facing the biggest crisis of my life, he'd saved me yet again, in a way. He'd given me a baby. He'd given me a future.

At the end of the month, I'd move out of my apartment and started living at his parents' house. I just knew that, with their help and companionship, we'd most definitely give my child a happy life.

I sat up and took out the thermos from my tote bag. It was the Snoopy one I'd received as a keepsake.

As I drank the barley tea I'd poured into my cup, a tear fell from my eye.

The sun was shining through the gaps in the branches overhead. A soft light enveloped me, as if conveying some message from the heavens.

Chapter 2
To My Father, I Say

The puck bounced off the wall of the table and flew into the goal box on my side. The scoreboard overhead ticked from 8–8 to 8–9.

"Argh, dammit!"

I flung my mallet onto the table, but deep down, I wasn't the least bit bitter. In fact, I didn't actually care if I won or lost. I just did that to show my mentor, Mr. Hatakeyama, that I was taking air hockey seriously. That I meant business.

I put the puck back on the table. It hovered over the surface through the gushing air, and I hit it with my mallet—but I overshot my serve, and the puck fell off the table.

"Ah, sorry about that!"

Scratching my head, I went to pick up the puck, which had rolled toward the bowling alley. I wanted to go home soon. There was no way an air hockey match could be any fun when played with folks who were this exhausting to be around. What's more, our opponents were big shots from the manufacturer we had to do business with. It was already tough enough to be on the same team as Mr. Hatakeyama, but I was fussing over so many little things that I was scared to death of screwing something up.

Mr. Hatakeyama snatched the puck I'd retrieved, not disguising his dislike of me in the least. He then placed the puck on the table and turned his attention to the right-hand wall. I thought he was going to ricochet it from there, but instead, he suddenly twisted his upper body and changed the trajectory of the mallet. The smash hit sank the puck straight into the opposing goal box.

"All right!" I shouted after seeing our score tick up to 9, before Mr. Hatakeyama himself could cry out in triumph. "Awesome feint!" I remarked, not meaning a word of it.

Mr. Hatakeyama's lips curled a tad, but the eyes behind his black-rimmed glasses weren't smiling. His face screamed, *Enough with the lame suck-up routine.*

"Match point! The game is heating up!"

The folks who'd already finished their match next to us surrounded the table. There were six of them, all new employees assigned to the same department at the same time.

My expression stiffened from nerves. Over the past two months since joining the workforce, all the attention I'd been drawing due to my string of screwups had proved traumatic.

Under the gazes of my fellow newbies, my right hand started shaking. I put too much strength in the mallet, and the puck I deflected fell off the table. I picked up the puck; everyone's eyes were fixed on me.

That flipped a switch in me, and I turned defiant. I struck the puck with all my might, and it traced a clean line directly into the opposing goal box.

"Yes! Whoooo!"

The elation of succeeding in front of so many eyes had me pumping my fist. My fellow newbies applauded me, too.

Mr. Hatakeyama, on the other hand, wasn't so pleased.

"A word, Sakamoto? Come here a sec. The rest of you, too."

After the two business partners we'd just beaten went to the bathroom, he called us over to the bowling alley's staircase.

"Listen, Sakamoto. We're here to entertain our esteemed partners, aren't we?"

"Yes, sir."

"And as such, we need to make sure they're having fun, wouldn't you agree? The whole reason we're spending the day drinking and bowling to begin with is to butter 'em up, isn't it? And that was the point of the air hockey game, too, *right*? So what are you doing, *winning the match*?!" he demanded, jabbing my chest with his finger. "You're supposed to make 'em look good! Didn't you notice how I was signaling you with my eyes earlier?"

I just stood stock-still there on the staircase's landing, unable to say anything.

"Hey, Tagano. What do you think?" Mr. Hatakeyama asked.

As our mentor, Mr. Hatakeyama was in charge of me and Tagano.

Tagano's narrow eyes fell on me, and he replied without the slightest hesitation, "Yeah, sir, if I were in Sakamoto's shoes at that moment, I would've lost on purpose."

"You would've, right, Tagano? I've been with the company for seven years, but it's been ages since I've seen somebody this clueless! Tch!"

Mr. Hatakeyama rushed over to the two business partners, who'd returned from the bathroom. "Let's drop by another place, shall we? It's Premium Friday, so let's not waste this opportunity. C'mon, guys, we'll all go together. Next up's a darts bar. You don't gotta worry about making the last train. We'll comp ya a cab!"

Tagano wasted no time whisking his great big frame to the elevators. "The elevator will be arriving shortly, gentlemen, so please follow me!" he said, beckoning them with a hand. Clearly, he was angling to be seen as someone with initiative.

"...I'm sorry, Mr. Hatakeyama. I'm going home," I told our mentor, loath as I was to say it, when he was the last one left waiting for the elevator.

"Excuse me?" He shot me a harsh look.

"Have a good night, sir," I said, bowing.

"Hold your horses!" he replied, but I'd already turned my back, fleeing down the stairs.

The train platform was dark and dead silent. I gulped down a can of whiskey and soda as I sat on the bench, and then I whipped out my phone to see a message from Shiho:

Sorry, can't make it to the movie tomorrow. Let's hit Shibuya some other time!

I didn't have the energy to ask why she couldn't come anymore. As things stood, my soul was too drained to go on dates with my girlfriend on my days off anyway.

Mr. Hatakeyama had sent me a photo of their guys at the darts bar through the group chat, too. He must've wanted to show me how they were enjoying themselves together, since I hadn't come along. The name of the group chat was *Hatakeyama and His Merry Mates*. (That was what he himself had titled it.)

I'd escaped to the nearest train station, but I couldn't muster the will to actually go home. I'd lost count of how many times Mr. Hatakeyama had yelled at me that one night. When I was pouring beer for someone, he said I had to keep the label facing outward. When we were raising our glasses for a toast, he told me to keep my glass slightly lower than my superiors'. He got on my case over the smallest stuff. Just thinking about the wining and dining we'd be doing next week gave me a sinking feeling.

There were several other office workers on the platform bench drinking cans of beer. Back when I was in school, I used to wonder why these people didn't just go home and drink, but now I could relate. They were savoring some alone time. I was sure that when they got home, their families would hit them with lectures and complaints. Maybe they'd get into arguments with their wives about their kids' education. But when they were by themselves at the dimly lit platform drinking a beer, they could forget about all that. That had to be it.

When I was in college, I could choose whoever was most convenient for me to hang out with. If I didn't like somebody, I didn't have to bother with them. But not anymore.

I was staring blankly at a passing train when my phone rang—a friend from my college tennis club. I wanted to ignore it, but the phone just kept ringing, so I reflexively picked up.

"*Hey, Sakamoto. Long time no see. You doing good?*"

"'Course I am, bro. Right now, I'm at a darts bar with my fellow newbies at the company. Playing darts is pretty fun, gotta say."

I got up out of my seat so the people around me wouldn't overhear.

"Where you working again? Marunouchi?"

"Yeah, a huge Marunouchi building. But anyway, what's up?"

"Well, I mean, these days, you never pick up when I call ya. Me and the guys from tennis club have been talking about getting together for drinks, so I thought I'd invite your ass, too."

"Sorry. Lately, it's been one work bender after the other. Lemme tell ya, man, a trading conglomerate's really where it's at. They let me eat like a king every night."

"You still going steady with Shiho?"

"Yeah, of course, bro. We're gonna go shopping in Shibuya tomorrow. Sorry, it's my turn to throw darts. Call ya later."

I hung up. I kicked myself for putting up a front like that.

I'm pathetic.

An intense wave of self-hatred washed over me. When we graduated college, I told my tennis buddies, *"Let's see who brings in the most dough! I'll have you guys beat—just you wait and see!"* After such a dramatic declaration, I could hardly tell them how rough I was doing.

I sat back down, and while I was downing some more whiskey and soda, my phone rang again. This time, it was Dad. No way I could bring myself to take *this* call. I waited for it to go to voicemail.

"Hello? You there, Yuuichi? It's your father. The lawn's gettin' overgrown; care to come help me mow it? When can you come back to Yugawara? Gimme a ring."

I heaved a sigh. It was only an innocent request. Sure, he'd just turned sixty, but he could still do garden work by himself, couldn't he?

I'd been living alone in Tokyo since starting college. My folks lived in Yugawara, and I hadn't seen them a single time since my big sister's wedding over a year ago. They sent bags of rice to my apartment once a month, but currently, that was our sole interaction. I never reached out to them of my own accord.

I'd looked down on my father for a long time. He worked for a small, local building contractor as a blue-collar laborer, always in his filthy fatigues. He'd shown up on parents' day at my school wearing dirt-caked clothing. And when I was in high school, he'd clean the gutters near campus and occasionally do repairs in my school building. I didn't want my classmates thinking of him as my father, so I'd even pretended not to know him.

I'd solemnly sworn to myself that I'd never be like him. I used him as an example of what not to do. I studied till I dropped and managed to get into a famous private university in Tokyo, eventually realizing my heart's desire and snagging a job at a famous trading company with an average annual income of twelve million yen.

But now look at me.

Disoriented from the whiplash between my current workplace and my college days, my incompetence was being thrust in my face on a daily basis.

Looking at the darts-bar photo tanked my mood even further.

The office phone was ringing, and my heart jumped, my body violently freezing up. I really hated taking calls at work. Inwardly, I hoped somebody else would pick it up in my stead, but the other employees on the sales floor were tied up with other tasks. Plus, the phone was closest to my desk, so it made the most sense for me to grab it, unfortunately.

"Hello, you've reached Yamano Corporation's Food Materials Department. Sakamoto speaking."

"*<Hello. This is John Clemens from World Foods Corporation.>*"

The stream of fluent English made me tense. Obviously, as a trading company, we got frequent calls from overseas. During my training, they'd made me role-play taking calls in English many times, but I still wasn't used to it.

"<I—I am sorry, to wh-who is speaking?>" I asked in halting English.

I'd lost my bearings, causing me to forget his name. He said his name again, but his tone was a bit biting. I got flustered, and the screws in my head flew loose, leaving me in a state of disarray.

"<S-sorry—Mr. John Clemens, errr, how—how can I be help to—?>"

Tagano, who was behind me taking a meeting, picked up the phone without waiting for me to finish. As if to flaunt that he was a cut above me, he demonstrated his command of English. He'd studied English literature in college, so he was quite fluent.

Our fellow newbies, who were typing away at their desks nearby, chuckled in response. Mr. Hatakeyama was drinking some coffee in a corner and sending a withering look my way. *This sucks.*

Later that night, Mr. Hatakeyama took me and Tagano to an *izakaya* bar not far from work.

"So anyway, when are you gonna finally learn how to take a call, Sakamoto?" Mr. Hatakeyama demanded.

We were seated at a low table over a sunken bit of the floor. Mr. Hatakeyama downed a glass of beer in the seat in front of me. I went to pour him some more, only for his expression to sour again.

"How many times do I have to tell you?! When pouring for someone else, keep the bottle's label facing up!"

"Ah, sorry, sir."

I shifted in discomfort, and my legs bumped into Mr. Hatakeyama's under the table.

"Ah, sorry, sir," I repeated under my breath.

"And another thing. I've been meaning to bring this up, but could you stop it with all the 'ah, sorry, sir's? It's a real verbal tic of yours. That 'ah,' I mean. It gets under my skin, so quit it, would ya?"

"Ah, sorry, sir."

"Come *on*, pal, you hit me with another 'ah' *immediately*?!" he said, gunning for laughs.

He shot a meaningful look at the nearby Tagano, who clapped his hands and laughed, though I very much doubted any of that was sincere. Meanwhile, I wasn't laughing. I couldn't even force a mere smile. Not when I was the butt of the joke.

Mr. Hatakeyama had hated me from the start. At our company, new hires underwent a thorough training course from the moment they started until the end of the Golden Week holidays. Mr. Hatakeyama had assumed the responsibility of instructor, and whenever he'd spout the occasional zinger, the hundred-plus new hires would all laugh in unison. To me, the sight of them forcing themselves to laugh in order to be liked gave me the skin-crawling impression of a chorus of religious devotees. I'd been seated all the way in the front that day and remained stone-faced. That must have been when Mr. Hatakeyama started having it out for me. From that point onward, he'd throw hard-to-answer questions my way during the training period in order to humiliate me.

What's more, the department I got assigned to after the training period was none other than his: Food Materials. He was one of the top salesmen there, and unfortunately for me, he became my mentor. I tried backpedaling, forcing myself to laugh at his inane excuses for jokes, but it was too late. He treated Tagano, who seemed to have more going for him, with warmth, and me with undisguised coldness.

"Well, anyhow, I've got one thing I wanna say to you, Sakamoto," Mr. Hatakeyama began as he pushed up his glasses and downed some more of his beer. "If ya wanna stick around, just don't make me hate you. Hold on, bathroom break." He got up out of his seat.

"I'll get you another beer, sir," Tagano said instantly, also rising from his seat.

"You're always so thoughtful, ain't ya, Tagano?" Mr. Hatakeyama replied.

Tagano shot me a condescending look.

"Tell me, Tagano," I said after Mr. Hatakeyama disappeared behind the restroom door, "don't you get tired living like that?"

"Sorry?"

"I'm asking if fawning over every single person you meet doesn't get exhausting."

"How about you give it a shot yourself instead of crying about it?"

I didn't reply.

"What's wrong with sucking up to people? As an employee at a trading company, I've decided that my priority at this stage is networking."

"Don't go thinking you're hot shit just 'cause you can speak good English. Schmucks like you who suck up all day really piss me off."

"I don't wanna hear that from a liability like you."

I had no response to that. In order to drown my frustrations, I drained the whiskey and soda in my mug.

"God, he's a real piece of work, ain't he? That Tagano."

I plopped myself onto a chair and cracked open the can of distilled *shochu* with tonic water on the round table—my fifth can that night.

"You've been so quiet. What do *you* think, Shiho?"

My girlfriend had come to my apartment in Adachi to hang out. I'd met her while I was hunting for a job. We'd both been busy with work recently, so this was our first time together in a month.

"I mean, I'm not gonna generalize or anything," she replied, "but I don't think he's completely wrong, per se."

I'd been fishing for a vote of agreement, only to get slapped with a full-on no.

"Why are you taking *his* side?" I said, brow furrowed.

"I'm not taking anybody's side. I just get his point of view that cultivating connections is important. And I don't think there's anything wrong with getting somebody to like you in order to get work!" she replied triumphantly, narrowing her big eyes.

Ever since she'd entered the workforce, Shiho had really started making her opinions heard loud and clear. She'd scored a position with a prospect of promotion at a major apparel company. Right when we'd landed our jobs, we'd grabbed a meal alongside Tagano once or twice.

"Your problem is," she continued, "you're too conceited for your own good."

"Excuse me?"

"The pride you feel in graduating from a good college is getting in the way of your work life. I think once you're on the job, your academic background stops mattering."

"Ah, shut it, princess."

"Don't talk to me that way. Sorry, but I have to get up early tomorrow, too, so I'm going home."

She stood up, and I caught a view of the many thick business books in her bag. It was like I was being confronted with just how different our mentalities were, and she felt oceans away from me as a person.

"You moron!" Mr. Hatakeyama shouted at the otherwise-empty landing of the emergency staircase. "These files contain trade secrets! The hell are you doing, taking 'em home with you?!"

"I'm sorry, sir!"

"You know we've got regulations to uphold, don't ya? You're fine because I happened to notice, but under different circumstances, you'd have faced disciplinary action!"

"I'm truly sorry, sir!"

I was pale in the face, down on my knees before the furious Mr. Hatakeyama while the cicadas cried in the background.

Last night, when I was working overtime alone on the floor, I noticed some documents in the trash can by Mr. Hatakeyama's desk. I picked up the whole bundle, and looking through it, I found a wealth of info on sales marketing know-how and effective sales methods. I was anxious and impatient, as a colleague in my year at our division had already taken over the work of one of their seniors and was making the rounds with customers on their own. I was falling behind my peers, so I figured I'd bone up more on sales myself.

"I'm really, really sorry, sir. I was thinking of studying at home in preparation for when I start going places on business."

"I've got no intention of letting you go anywhere, buddy boy!"

Those words deflated me.

"Besides, if you wanna study, do it here in the office! Don't take that stuff home!"

He was absolutely right, but I couldn't do that. In the office, I couldn't concentrate because I always felt like I was being watched by the people around me—the same reason I struggled with answering the phones. I always shrank in on myself, and my voice would start quavering.

"I swear. We're so busy preparing for the exhibition at the end of the month, too. I'm choosing not to report this to the chief. If they find out, they'll chew me out, too. You owe me one, kiddo."

Mr. Hatakeyama clicked his tongue and returned to the office. I also returned, and I tried to hand over the copy of the document that a senior colleague had asked me for. However, since it was my first time working with someone from another department, I couldn't remember who'd asked me to do it. Lack of sleep had me all muddleheaded. On top of working a ton of overtime and entertaining business partners day after day, I'd been coming to work at six thirty in the morning daily as of late, making use of the empty floor to practice taking phone calls.

"I have your copy, sir!"

"I didn't ask for one."

"I have your copy, sir!"

"Wasn't me, either."

I went around asking people, the bundle of files tucked under my arm, but I couldn't find my person.

"You asked me for a copy, right, sir?"

"Wasn't me."

"Your copy, sir!"

"Wasn't me."

"Sakamoto!" Mr. Hatakeyama shouted loudly enough for everyone on the floor to hear. "It's Mr. Sakuragi in Financial Affairs who wants that copy!"

The people around me were chuckling, as if to say, *Another day, another blunder with that guy, huh?*

When I returned to my desk, the Food Materials Department phone rang. My desire to show off the results of my training wrestled with my hope that somebody would take the call instead. In the end, the more fired-up half of me won out.

"Hello, this is Yamano Corporation's Food Materials Department, Sakamoto speaking."

"*<Hello.>*"

The second I heard the English, my brain went blank.

"<H-hello. How—how—how do I help you th-th-this afternoon? What? Er, uhhh, can—can you say, uh, th-that agai—?>"

In the middle of the conversation, the receiver flew out of my left hand. I fearfully turned to look; Mr. Hatakeyama was holding the phone, rage in his eyes.

I was at the wheel of a company car, driving down the dark and silent Shuto Expressway. Another vehicle was on the road, a car with a large surfboard on its roof. Unable to keep their impatience in check, the driver cut me off from the right-hand lane.

Hitting a toll-road rest stop on the weekend had become a new routine for me. I liked the atmosphere at a rest stop when it was the dead of night. Drinking coffee on one of the benches outside was the only time I was able to shake free of the unpleasantness.

As I gazed at the evenly spaced orange panel lights, memories of what had happened since I started work flashed through my mind:

"You dumbass!"

"No, you twit!"

"How many times do I have to say it before it penetrates your thick skull?"

In the four months since I joined the company, I'd only ever gotten yelled at. Even when I did a good job, I never heard a peep of praise. Because in this world, being capable was supposed to come naturally.

As I gripped the steering wheel, I found myself wishing for a traffic accident to grant me a swift death. I was half-seriously contemplating just closing my eyes and letting go for ten seconds when my phone started ringing from the passenger seat. Dad's name lit up on the screen. I kept ignoring his constant calls, letting them go to voicemail.

"Hello? It's your father. I bought a new computer, but I ain't very good with the things. Could ya drop by during the Obon holidays 'n' show me how to work it? Call me back."

"Look it up your own damn self," I blurted out.

My dad was still using a flip phone. He was largely ignorant when it came to tech in general, and he had zero skill as a businessman. I felt the urge to take him to task, because honestly, what if the reason I wasn't doing too hot at work was because I inherited his incompetence?

"Mr. Hatakeyama, if I may have a moment of your time."

Me and my coworkers were in a large conference room on the first floor of our workplace. While we had our hands full late at night preparing for the exhibition, Tagano was huddled up with Mr. Hatakeyama, who was looking over the handouts.

"What is it, Tagano?"

"Might it be a good idea to staple the visitors' business cards and survey forms after tomorrow's exhibition? I think having the information organized that way will help the business discussions flow more smoothly."

"You're right. Always thinking ahead, eh, Mr. Future Company President?" Mr. Hatakeyama teased, talking into his hand as if it were a megaphone.

"Oh, no, you flatter me," said Tagano. Then he spouted a line that really made my blood boil: "I'd simply hate to sully a project organized by my esteemed mentor."

I was in no mood to propose something like Tagano had. When Mr. Hatakeyama became my mentor, he'd instructed me to start acting on my own initiative, but if I actually did that, all of a sudden, it became *"Don't do these things without consulting anyone!"*

Ever since then, I got made fun of as a drudge who just waited for orders, but at this point, I was fine with that.

I stayed in a corner of the floor so nobody noticed me, counting the number of paper cups. The next day, we'd be running an exhibition at a trade partner's location in Marunouchi. It was a corporation rolling out a chain of home-improvement retailers, and items purchased by the Food Materials Department were slated to be displayed in the company's meeting space. Everything was being prepared at our building; the goods would be loaded onto a truck and brought over in the morning.

While I was checking the number of paper plates (to be used for samples), Tagano came up next to me. "How's Shiho doing? She go someplace for the Obon break?"

"Mind your own business."

I hadn't seen Shiho in a while. Every time I called her during days off, she'd turn me down, saying she had a seminar to attend. We texted each other often enough, but our conversations never went anywhere.

"Already eleven, huh?" Mr. Hatakeyama set his eyes on his expensive-looking watch. "All right, that's enough for today. We've got an early start tomorrow. We'll do the nitty-gritty stuff after we get to the location. You folks can go home."

The other newbies excused themselves, exiting the room one after the other. I was about to leave as well, but Mr. Hatakeyama stopped me.

"You hold on a second, Sakamoto. We need to have a word."

After making sure everyone was gone, he called me to the back of the conference room. Scowling, he whipped off the cloth concealing the signboard on the floor. It was a rectangular foam panel that was going to be suspended from the ceiling at the exhibition venue. The center of the signboard had a dent in it; the panel had been pierced through, and the entire sheet with the text had crumpled from the impact.

"You did this, didn't you?" he demanded, glaring at me sharply.

"Huh?"

"You're the one who stepped on this, ain't ya?"

"I did no such thing!" I insisted.

But he kept at it, prodding me in the chest. "Who else could it possibly be?!"

"It was you, wasn't it?" I said. "Did *you* do this?"

I noticed bits of Styrofoam stuck to the hem of his right pants leg, which I brought to his attention. While it took some courage to talk back, I couldn't simply grin and bear this. Not when somebody was trying to pin something on me.

"So what if I did?" he replied coolly.

I was speechless.

His expression eased up. "Remember that one time you left carrying restricted-access files?"

I said nothing.

"That's no small offense. Of course, as your mentor, I'm responsible for you, too. But however new you may be to the company, you've been one big train of mistakes since you joined. That, combined with the grave matter of the files…"

He didn't have to elaborate. I understood what he was getting at. He wanted me to pretend *I* wrecked the sign. That was what was written all over his face as he triumphantly piled that crap on me.

I was so beyond angry and disgusted that it crossed over into just being sad. Sad an asshole like him was my mentor, and sad that this company let such trash go unchecked just because their business performance was top-level.

"You're scum, sir. You know that, right?" I spat.

I struck the nearby brochure-display stand hard. Then I turned to leave. Mr. Hatakeyama shouted abuse at me from behind, but I ignored him and exited the building.

At the station platform, I bought a beer from the vending machine. Wanting somebody to vent to, I sat on the bench and called Shiho, the beer can in my other hand.

"Sorry, I'm out bowling with people from work."

I heard giggly, coquettish voices in the background of the call.

"What're you doing, Shiho, babe?" came the voice of one of her male coworkers. *"You're up next."*

Why was this guy calling her "babe"? I got a sense of how good the interpersonal relations must've been at her workplace, filling me with misery.

She hung up before I could even get a word in. Then I got a notification. When I opened the app with a depressed look on my face, I saw it was about new messages in the *Hatakeyama and His Merry Mates* group chat.

Thanks for another day's hard work, Mr. Hatakeyama. Let's do our best tomorrow~~

Thank you so much for all your guidance today and every day, Mr. Hatakeyama! Looking forward to working with you tomorrow, too!

The messages were pouring in, each employee competing to thank him faster than the rest. Before long, Mr. Hatakeyama himself chimed in.

Good work today, everybody! Bad news—the signboard got a dent in it! Which one of you stepped on it?! lol. Oh well. It's not my style to chew out my adorable little newbies. We don't have the time to order a replacement, so I'll just pretend that I broke it and take the heat for it from the department chief. We meet at the office at 6:30 tomorrow! We'll survive without the signboard, so let's do this thing!

The second that appeared:

Best mentor ever!

Your kindness is god-tier, Mr. Hatakeyama!

The responses pinged in one after the other.

Still wrapped up in an abiding gloom, I staggered onto the last train of the day. A tired-looking office worker was hanging on to one of the nearby ceiling straps.

Back when I was enjoying college life, I thought worn-out corporate slaves like that man were boring losers just going through the motions. But not anymore. *Corporate guys are incredible.* The kind of mental fortitude it took to withstand all the ridiculous BS was, in my eyes, downright inhuman.

I noticed my reflection in the train window. I couldn't do a damn thing at work, but hey, at least my tie was tied properly. What a grown-up I must be, right? Ha. A laughable sight if ever there was one.

Loneliness stabbed me and put my heart in a vise. The dark landscape passing by outside the window was registering as *scary*, somehow. I didn't have a lick of confidence I could continue working at this rate. The tipsiness certainly wasn't helping, but due to my hazy but real anxiety regarding the future, I suddenly found myself wanting to die.

I didn't go to work the following morning.

Nor the morning after. Nor the morning after that. Nor the morning after that morning.

A text from Shiho: Let's see other people.

I couldn't get out of my futon. I didn't have the energy to ask her why. I simply answered, Okay.

I quit my job.

There was no handover of work or anything. I basically just disappeared.

I'd lasted only five months at the company. And that was how my dream of living the high-earning, high-powered trading-company-employee life came to an end.

I started another job in October. A temp-agency job in Tokyo. I just wanted a normal office job. My experience working at a trading company had left me traumatized, and I figured that pushing papers at a desk would mean less of those onerous interpersonal relationships. Thanks to my academic background and the fact that the agency made some allowance for recent graduates looking to change jobs, I was able to pivot without any trouble.

Yet I didn't even last a month there.

The whole time I sat at my desk, I felt *watched*. My nerves were so frayed that if I heard someone laughing somewhere, I couldn't help but feel like it was *me* they were laughing at. I couldn't calm down and keep working unless I got up and walked to the source to make absolutely sure I hadn't been the butt of it.

Nobody yelled at me, but it took very little to deflate my spirits regardless. For example, when someone who used to reply to e-mails with *got it!* started replying *got it* without the exclamation point, my mind would go blank: *Do they hate me now?*

Whenever the phone at my desk rang, I got up out of my seat in fear, too afraid to take the call. There was no way a company could hire somebody like me. I ended up leaving the company in a way that was a hairbreadth away from receiving the pink slip.

After I quit the temp-agency job, I received a voicemail from my dad at the end of October.

"Hello? It's your old man. I got my hands on tickets to a Japan Series game, so how 'bout we go check it out together? They're the box seats behind the backstop. Gimme a ring."

I ignored that message from him, same as always. I'd never called him back. Not even once. I hadn't told my parents I'd quit the trading company, either.

Back when I graduated from the big-name university in Tokyo, this was what I'd told them:

"You can bet your asses I'm gonna land a job at a huge company and become a big shot! I'm gonna join a huge trading company and climb all the way to president, so watch me!"

"You don't have to grind yourself to dust like that, Yuuichi," my mom had replied. *"Just get into any old company, and that'll be enough."*

But I looked down on my blue-collar dad so much that I said, *"That ain't gonna cut it, Mom. There's no point working if you don't rake in the big bucks!"*

I'd gotten so full of myself without anything to base that confidence on. And you'd better believe I opened my big mouth to boast up a storm when I landed that job. To tell the truth, part of me wanted to just cry into their arms. But I couldn't.

Right after the New Year, I moved to a place far from the city center. When I was at the trading company, the company paid my rent, but now that I was unemployed, I couldn't pay my bills, so I started living in a small closet-sized apartment. I didn't want my parents to know I'd moved, so I chose an apartment that didn't require a guarantor.

Also, I had the post office help me forward to my new place the rice my parents would send every month. Thankfully, beginning in autumn of the year prior, they'd also sent me some other food, allowing me to eke out a meager life (together with the modest savings I'd accumulated during my time pulling in money at the trading company).

By mid-January, I was working part-time at a nearby convenience store. But I didn't last a single week there. I thought I might be able to survive at a part-time job, but it was the very act of interacting with other people that had me deathly afraid. If a customer started nagging at me about something, I'd feel like they hated me as a person, and my hands would start trembling over the cash register.

Staying home did little to soothe my nerves. Whenever my phone made a noise, my body shuddered at the thought that somebody from my trading-company days was calling me. And when I was out and about, I was too scared to pass through any places or roads I'd been to even just once during my job from hell. Whenever I visited the city center for a change of pace, I couldn't bring myself to take one step closer to the Marunouchi district.

Wanting somebody to vent to, I'd looked through my phone contacts, but I couldn't find anyone I wanted to see, and that was because it was so easy to imagine becoming even more dispirited when I met them. This person led a fulfilling work life, so if we hung out, I'd just end up comparing myself with them. *This* person had a girlfriend, so I'd just boil with envy, and *this* person, when talking to somebody less fortunate than them, would act like they had no ill will yet do their best to make them feel even worse. Meanwhile, this other person would pretend to give you well-meaning advice but just use the opportunity to flaunt their knowledge of psychology, so they were right out.

But everyone in my list of contacts seemed positively radiant compared with my current wretched state. I couldn't find anybody on my wavelength, and ultimately, I had no choice but to hole myself up in my home as a shut-in.

A tepid gust blew from the floodplain of the Edo River. I took off my thin windbreaker, tucked it under my arm, and scanned the passbook in my hand.

Checking my balance at the ATM of a large shopping mall in my neighborhood was a new daily ritual for me. At the end of January, two hundred thousand yen was transferred to my bank account under the name of *KRLB*. Was that the Kanto Region Labor Board or something?

People who quit their jobs within one year of graduation weren't eligible for unemployment insurance. While I did wonder if this windfall was the result of some error, I couldn't help but hold out hope that I'd be receiving another deposit in the same vein. But reality was a harsh mistress. Miracles like that weren't exactly common, and I had precious little money left.

I entered the mall to buy a cheap bento and hurry home. Since it was a Saturday, even though it was in the evening, places were packed with parents and their families.

I spotted a bargain corner for food at a supermarket near the mall's entrance. Inside the large steel wagon lay tall piles of loaves of bread with half-off stickers slapped on them. I hadn't eaten anything since around noon the day before. I pushed aside the crowd and slipped past them, my bloodshot eyes scanning for sustenance. I grabbed a thick cutlet sandwich almost at the same time as an old person next to me, but I ripped it out of his hands. I knew no shame, and I had no pride. Not anymore.

It happened when I turned to grab a half-off bento. I spotted Shiho walking from the direction of the entrance, her arm happily locked with a tall man's. When I saw his face, my heart skipped a beat. It was Tagano.

When we first joined Yamano Corporation, I'd once gone to visit Tagano at his place (he'd lived alone) with Shiho. His apartment wasn't far from this mall.

I was so distraught that I couldn't even remember where I was. Whatever crumb of composure I had left allowed me to blend back into the crowd.

The two entered the bakery across from the supermarket. Tagano quickly picked up one of the trays and placed pieces of bread onto it using the provided tongs; clearly, he was familiar with that specific place's layout. All the bread at that bakery cost upward of three hundred yen apiece. Whenever I visited this mall, the fragrant aroma hit my nostrils; I'd have loved to eat some of that small but delicious bread one day. But I had to settle for the bread that was the biggest and cheapest.

There I was, in the supermarket inside the mall, my crumpled and unappetizing cutlet sandwich in my hand. My sandwich that cost ninety yen. My sandwich that I'd stolen from an elderly person who was presumably scraping by on a pension.

The despair that suffused my heart felt fathomless. I cast my eyes downward, frozen to that spot.

Suddenly, the phone in the back pocket of my jeans started vibrating. Since the call-incoming ringtone filled me with fear, I'd put it on vibrate instead. And the vibrating in my jeans pocket just wouldn't stop, no matter how long I ignored it, so I reluctantly took it out. Mom's name was on the screen.

I don't even care what happens anymore. Spurred by an emotion not unlike defiance, I answered the call for the first time in ages.

She was weeping, sobbing. *"Yuuichi. Yuuichi…"*

"What's the matter, Mom?"

"It's your father. He's dead."

"Huh?"

"Your father died in the train derailment this morning!"

"……"

The giant jumble of information knocked around inside my head, and I couldn't sort my thoughts.

"Drop everything and come to Minami-Kamakura Gymnasium."

Utterly confused, I did as my mother told me to and ran out of the shopping mall.

The service entrance to the gymnasium was covered with a large blue tarp. At the urging of a police officer, I entered through the gap in the blue sheet they peeled open for me.

The moment I crossed the passage into the court, the atmosphere morphed into something alien to me. An oppressively heavy and dense air pervaded the room, and sobs and wails could be heard from every which way.

"Yuuichi!"

My sister was waving me over from a corner of the court. I ran up to her to find Mom sitting on the floor, sniffling. My father was laid out face up on a mat on the floor. His face was surprisingly clean, and while his suit jacket was torn, I didn't see any obvious external wounds anywhere.

"Apparently, they examined his body a little while ago and determined he hit his head bad," my sister's husband told me. He put a hand on my shoulder from behind.

With a solemn look on his face, he continued: They were able to identify my father immediately because he had his driver's license in his wallet. I'd learned about the derailment on my phone while I was in the taxi en route to the gymnasium. To think Dad had been aboard that train…

I knelt down and held his hand. The watch on his left wrist was shattered, evidence of the impact of the crash.

It had been two years since my sister's wedding, which was the last time I had seen my father. I hadn't seen him in ages; it added to why I felt like this accident almost had nothing to do with me. I was cornered in both my professional and private life, and my heart had been squeezed dry of feeling.

No matter how hard I gripped his now-clammy hand, in a cruel twist of fate, the tears would not flow.

A red-faced salaryman was sitting on the station-platform bench I always used. I was a bit miffed. It felt like somebody had usurped the only place I could know peace.

On the heels of the memorial service held forty-nine days after my father's death—as was customary—I returned to Tokyo. My sister had taken the lead in dealing with the aftermath. Even after all this time, I had yet to tell my family that I'd quit my job. Right after the funeral, I went back to my Tokyo apartment. (*"Work at the trading company's crazy busy right now."*)

"Okay, application form complete!"

Next to me on the bench, students in their best hire-me suits were filling out paperwork. They were all whining about how fed up they were with job hunting, but they still had life in their eyes.

They shone as bright as the sun to me. Two years ago, I'd had that same spark in my eyes. I'd also been fed up with the job-hunting paperwork I had to fill out over and over again, but I'd told myself I'd be making a hundred million yen. As I reminisced about those days, something my father had told me sprang to mind.

During my job-hunting period, he'd called me incessantly to impart me with everything he knew about the proper attire, interview etiquette, and so on. In this day and age, information like that was an internet search away, and I took part in plenty of mock interviews during college. Every time he called, I replied to the effect of *"Yeah, no duh, Dad, I already know that."*

But my father didn't relent. When I applied for a job at Yamano Corporation, I got voicemails from him with info on the company.

"Your old man here. I looked into Yamano, so let me tell ya what I dug up. They've got three thousand five hundred employees, but when ya count the groups and subsidiaries and things, it's over fifty thousand. They've got a hundred and thirty billion in capital—"

Back then, I hated it. It was so annoying. But he'd just been looking out for his son, same as any father would. In hindsight, I felt guilty.

The winds from the hill road carried a stifling sulfur smell. I passed rows of wooden *ryokan* inns and tourists in yukata as I walked up the hill.

One day in May, I figured I'd burn some of the time on my hands by returning to Yugawara. Surrounded by mountains on all sides, this hot-spring town hadn't changed one bit from back when I was a kid. I visited every one of my old stomping grounds. It was a stroll down memory lane.

I turned down a side street to go to my parents' house and happened by a gaggle of elementary school students on their way home. They set their distinctive grade-school leather backpacks on the floor and soaked their feet in the footbath on the side of the road.

"Hey, you hear the rumors about the ghost train?" asked one of their number, a chubby kid whose eyes were sparkling with adventure.

"No, I haven't. What rumors?"

"You remember how that train derailed, right? Well, they say if you visit Nishi-Yuigahama Station late at night, you'll see the train that ran on that day."

"No *way*!"

Kids were innocent, and that was a good thing. When I was a kid, before I got jaded, I believed in spooky stuff like that, too. Oh, to go back to those days. Now I was jealous of the grade-schoolers who could shoot the breeze so happily like that.

Down a side street was the building contractor company my father used to work for. Solar panels had been installed on its tiled roof, and from the outside, it looked like any old private house. The sign hanging on the wall of the second floor looked about ready to crash down any moment.

"Hey, you don't happen to be Mr. Sakamoto's son, do ya?"

A white-haired man pulled open the building's brown sash door.

"That's me," I replied.

He grinned and stepped outside. "That crash was terrible, just terrible."

I saw this man at my father's funeral. He'd been crying the whole time, handkerchief in hand. During my high school years, he'd come with my father to my school to make repairs. If I remembered correctly, his name was Mr. Takenaka.

"Yuuichi, right? Are you feeling a bit better?" he asked me.

"Yes, thankfully. I'm sorry my father's passing caused you so much trouble."

"Don't be a stranger, Yuuichi. I can't tell ya how much your old man helped me out when he worked for me. I respect him more than anybody in the whole wide world."

Hearing those words of praise, my heart became fraught with emotion.

"But never mind that, Yuuichi, I hear you're working for Yamano? That's amazing!"

"Yeah, uh, it's, you know...," I said evasively.

"You were Mr. Sakamoto's pride and joy. He was beyond delighted when you got into that college. I'd never seen such a happy look on his face before then!"

"...What kind of person was he? You know, in the workplace?"

I wanted to know more about my father.

"There's no end to all the good things I could list about the guy. One, he never, ever threw in the towel. Around this time last year, after a big typhoon hit Yugawara, he spent night after night repairing destroyed houses. The damage some areas suffered was catastrophic, but Mr. Sakamoto played a central role in building those places back up. It wasn't as though working that hard would earn him more money, but once he set his mind on something, you better believe he'd get it done!"

I said nothing.

"Also, he was incredibly dutiful. With his skills, he could easily have headed to the big city to earn more. Heck, had I been in his shoes, I'm certain I would've done just that. But not him, no sir. He was always saying he'd hate to abandon the folks in town. I only had eight employees, and without Mr. Sakamoto, I'm worried about the future and then some."

He looked up at the sky above. Every one of those tidbits was news to me. I wanted to hear more about my father, but just then a little old lady came from a side road pushing a stroller. I remembered her; she'd repeatedly bowed her wrinkled head as she faced my father's coffin during the funeral.

"You're the Sakamotos' boy, aren't you?" As soon as she saw me, she grasped my hand tight, smiling. "You're the spitting image of your father, young man. I'm so indebted to him, I can't even count all the ways I owe him!"

She finally let go of my hand, staring off into the distance.

"Your father was a truly kind soul. Not only did he fix my toilet, but he also cleaned my garden while he was at it, free of charge! Whenever he had the time, he'd come running to my place to keep me company since I live alone. That man… He was my hero, plain and simple."

Hearing her get choked up, a fuzzy feeling spread inside me.

The funeral had played host to quite the long line of mourners. Everyone in attendance had made sure to give Dad their heartfelt thank-yous as he lay in his coffin. Meanwhile, I'd looked down on my father for working a blue-collar job. How wrong I'd been.

The lush green grass was swaying in the wind in the distance ahead. When I was young, I'd practiced riding a bike with my father in this vacant lot. It took me a long time to get the hang of it, but Dad was always there with me anyway. Even on rainy days, and even on those days when work had left him exhausted.

I wanted to apologize to him. No, I *had* to apologize to him.

I passed through a residential area when everybody was asleep, and I arrived in front of Nishi-Yuigahama Station. I passed through the open ticket gate, the rumors those Yugawara grade-schoolers had talked about the day before fresh in my mind.

Those rumors had gained traction on the internet as well. I wasn't necessarily buying them, but I wanted to see my father again, no matter what that took, and that longing won out over my skepticism.

The platform was shrouded in darkness, and there was nobody else there. I took a seat on a bench and waited, but nothing happened for some time, so I headed to one of the vending machines for something to drink.

Just then, a translucent train started coming down the tracks toward me from the direction of Chigasaki Kaigan Station and stopped at the platform to the screech of the brakes. I caught my breath. There were more than a few passengers aboard.

The train door opened, revealing a girl in a high school uniform holding on to one of the ceiling straps.

"Go," she told a boy of small stature.

He seemed reluctant to get off, so she pushed him out the door. "Go already."

The high school girl came to the edge of the door. The two stared at each other for ages, as if they were loath to part ways.

"Thank you so much! I mean it—thank you!" The boy bowed his head deeply.

Just before the door closed, she smiled and said, "No, thank *you*, Kazuyuki."

The boy started heading toward the ticket gate; he gave me a nod when he noticed me. I got a closer glimpse of him as he passed by; his eyes were puffy from crying, but he had a satisfied look on his face.

"Would you also like to board the ghost train?" came a voice.

A different girl in a high school uniform appeared, walking toward me from the other end of the platform.

"...Are you a ghost?" I asked her.

"Sure am," she answered, her tone frank. "Pleased to meet you."

She started rattling off her lines, smoothly enough to make it clear she was used to it.

According to her, the train that had just passed was the very same train that had derailed in March. Only people with strong feelings regarding the disaster could see the train, and if one boarded it, they'd be able to see their loved one again.

"But there's a catch," she emphasized.

*   *   *

- You may board the train only from the station where the doomed rider first boarded.
- You mustn't tell the doomed rider that they are soon to die.
- You must get off the train at or before passing Nishi-Yuigahama Station. Otherwise, you, too, shall die in the accident.
- Meeting the doomed rider will not change their fate. No matter what you do, those who died in the accident will not come back to life. If you attempt to get people off the train before it derails, you will be returned to the present day.

Not long after she laid out the rules, I heard a thunderous *crash* far down the tracks.

"If you don't get off the train at some point, that'll be how *you* wind up, too," she said, smiling impishly. "If you're okay with nothing in reality changing, visit the station where your person boarded the train. You can go as soon as tomorrow night. Also," she continued, folding her arms as her gaze grew increasingly intense, "don't even think about getting your person off the train. I say that because a little while ago, I had a bereaved fiancée try that stunt."

My mind was made up. I didn't need my father to come back to life to want to do this. Reality didn't have to change one bit. I just wanted to see him again.

Nishi-Yugawara Station was covered in darkness. It was dead silent. I took my phone out of the pocket of my hoodie to check the time. That was when suddenly, light started to illuminate the whole platform. The clock on my phone went from the middle of the night to 10:23 in the morning.

I couldn't afford to waste time standing there slack-jawed over how the sun was now overhead. I spotted my father sitting on a bench in the back. Looking closer, I saw he had an old notebook of his open and that he was jotting something down. He'd been using that notebook for years and years. Just as I was about to approach him, a translucent train started pulling in.

The black train slowed to a stop. Dad boarded Car One, and I followed him through the same door.

This was the first station on the line, so there weren't many passengers yet. As the locomotive started moving, Dad took an aisle seat in the four-person box-seating area.

It'd take less than an hour for the train to reach Nishi-Yuigahama. Swallowing my panic, I stood beside him.

"Dad…," I said, my voice shrill with nerves.

My father glanced at me. He put the notebook in his hands into an old Boston bag and smiled. "That you, Yuuichi?"

"Why're you wearing a suit?"

"I'm on minor business."

Not wanting him to ask me what I was doing here, I replied, "I'm here on minor business, too."

He chuckled and tapped the seat across from him with his finger, prompting me to sit. While he'd always been slender, he looked a little thinner than I remembered him. But his arms were still muscular, as befitting a working man. You could tell he had impressive muscles even through the suit.

"Long time no see, huh?" he said to me.

I was so ashamed that it took courage to make eye contact. It had been two years since I'd seen him back at my sister's wedding. And even then, I'd barely talked to him. My job-hunting period had been just about to begin, and I'd given that all my attention. We hadn't engaged in a proper conversation since the New Year's break of the year before that. I felt so self-conscious, and I had no idea what to say.

He stared at me. At his awkward mess of a son. And he looked moved.

"…Uh, thanks for sending me that rice every month," I said, eyes downcast.

"Don't fret it."

"That rice is helping, kinda."

"I see."

A long pause from both of us.

"…You eating enough?" he asked.

"Yeah."

"Gotcha. Good, then."

Another awkward break in the conversation. My father was always a man of few words. Plus, we were both somewhat holding back out of consideration for the other. Thereby allowing silence to take hold.

"…You still a Hanshin Tigers fan?" he asked as we passed Enoura Station.

"'Course I am. What other baseball team could I possibly be into?" I replied grumpily.

He smiled with his whole face. Both he and I were big-time Tigers fans.

"When you were in elementary school, we used to watch matches at the ballpark all the time," he said in a nostalgic tone, folding his arms.

"We did, didn't we? At the Tokyo Dome, we were surrounded by an ocean of Giants fans. Remember how small we felt?"

"Yeah, I remember."

"Dad, you remember the foul ball that came flying during the Giants-Tigers match? Remember how it hit the beer you were holding and you got drenched?"

"Yep, that happened, too."

"Man, I had to laugh. I still think about that moment sometimes."

The mood in the air got a little less stiff. It was a relief, sensing the distance between us close like that. Even as we passed Odawarajou-mae, our small talk continued, the number of passengers steadily increasing all the while.

As we chatted over nothing much, I kept wondering with a sense of discomfort why he wasn't asking me about my job. Under normal circumstances, he'd almost certainly ask how work was treating me. We hadn't seen each other a single time since I'd entered the workforce, and as a father, how well I was doing at the company had to be on his mind.

Our chat was interspersed with long pauses. Even though it would have been easy to change the topic to work using those moments, he never brought it up.

"Looks like it's going to rain tomorrow," he said instead.

It was too unnatural. There was one explanation: He must have realized that I quit that job.

"Gotta say, though, it's nice being young. You can slip up, and it'll still work out in the end," he said suddenly, breaking from the flow of the conversation.

That random comment clinched it. He definitely knew. He was deliberately avoiding the topic of work out of consideration for my present predicament.

When I got into my high-level university, I'd talked real big to my parents. Real, real big. I told them I'd be a VIP. I told them to watch my meteoric rise, because I was going to join a big-name company and climb my way to the president's chair. Any normal person would have fired back with a *"Watch your rise," indeed* or *Turns out the working life's not so easy, huh?* But the man in front of me wasn't taking me to task in the least.

I thought about all the voicemails he'd left me after I started work. The message about him wanting to help with his garden. The message about needing help with his new computer. The message about his tickets to see a pro-baseball match. In hindsight, I realized those were all just excuses to see each other and talk.

"...Hey, Dad." The words came spilling out of my mouth. "I...haven't really done anything for you as a son...have I?"

I could no longer bring myself to look him in the face. For a while, guilt seized my heart, but then he stared at me with sharp eyes.

"If you regret your lack of filial piety, that's enough for me," he declared, a slight smile curling his lips.

I looked down. His dry, rough hands came into view. His thick, wrinkled fingers were covered in blisters, and there was dirt wedged in each of his fingernails. Those hands spoke volumes as to how hard he worked as a laborer.

And they were the hands that bought me my backpack for school.

The hands that paved my path to college.

Those sooty hands had made it possible for me to grow this big.

"Dad, I, uh..."

I wiped the tears that were blurring my vision and met his eyes.

"…I used to look down on your job. For a long time, on the inside. The way you're always working in dirty clothes made me think your job was lame and stupid. Then I started working myself, and I learned just how hard it is. I'm so sorry I ever regarded you as lesser. Forgive me."

I swallowed the sob that had climbed up my throat and continued, "I was wrong in every way. I'm sorry… I'm really sorry. Forgive me, Dad. I'm so sorry… I'm so, so sorry."

I bowed my head over and over again, choking up as I begged his forgiveness. Tears were rolling down my cheeks.

He just kept staring at me in silence. He didn't yell at me, but he didn't console me, either. He just folded his arms tight and stared, his eyes the tiniest bit bleary.

"I'm a giant loser," I said in disgust.

The second that came out of my mouth, Dad roared, "Don't be stupid! Anyone who comes to apologize over not doing enough as a son is no loser! Don't give me that nonsense!" He didn't seem to care that there were other passengers around to overhear. "Tell me, what's wrong with somebody studying hard and getting into a good college? And what's wrong with somebody who's kind enough to feel sorry over not being there for his parents? Don't let me hear you say something so ridiculous ever again!"

"……"

That was the first time my father had ever yelled at me. Since entering the workforce, I had felt the acute terror of getting shot down by others. But it was different coming from him. His words had punch, but they were full of love for his son.

"Besides, you're not weak. The ones who are truly weak can never be vulnerable in front of other people. You're a strong man, Yuuichi."

My tears flowed without end. They made Dad look blurry.

"Yuuichi. Do you remember when you were little and you used to practice riding a bike with your old man?"

I said nothing.

"You're a big klutz by nature, so it takes you more time than most when you try your hand at something. But once you get past that initial hump, you're the type that delivers twice the results other people do. That was true of when you finally got the hang of riding a bike, too. It took you some time to get there, but you never gave up. Whenever you fell down, you'd just keep getting back on your feet, time and again. You can do it. I know you can, because you're you. You can count on yourself."

He said that unfalteringly, with zero hesitation. The sheer power of his love for me buoyed my spirits, and I could feel strength coursing inside me.

Before I knew it, the train had passed Koiso Station.

"Dad… What sort of job do you think suits me?" I asked, after steadying my breathing.

"That's something you can never know until you actually try working there," he replied, "but if there's one thing I can say, I think you oughtta go for a job where you can feel the simple joy of hearing thank you from folks."

"'Thank you'?"

"Yep. That's what the working life's all about."

I didn't say anything.

"And if you want that for yourself, go meet lots of people. Never become a misanthrope. Because it's always other people who impart you with a purpose in life. It ain't computers, and it ain't machines. It's *people* who teach ya everything. So work up the courage and go interact with folks. Have a chat with lots and lots and lots of people."

I'd never had a conversation like this with my father. I wanted to talk to him more. I wanted to learn so much more from him. But the clock was ticking; over forty minutes had passed.

"Next stop, Chigasaki Kaigan. Chigasaki Kaigan Station."

The closer the train approached the station, the slower it got. My lips trembled at the thought of having to part ways.

"Enough now. Just get your butt out there." He grabbed me by the arm after it became clear I wasn't going to stand up and forced me to my feet. "Move it. Come on now."

I stood in front of the door. I couldn't look back, because if I saw his face again, I wouldn't be able to get off the train.

The train began to slow down rapidly. The *clack, clack* of the rails petered out, and the doors swung open.

Just as I was about to take a step outside, I heard him shout my name.

"Yuuichi!"

Hesitant as I was to do it, I slowly turned to look at my father.

"You're all grown-up."

His arms folded, he narrowed his eyes with satisfaction.

I got out of the train, and his eyes followed me through the window. I bit my lip hard, trying to stifle the tears.

I remembered seeing that look on Dad's face before, back when I was a little kid. I saw that same expression at the park, that one time…

The door slowly shut. The cold sea air was blowing in from the Chigasaki coastline. My tears blurred the sight of the train as it pulled out of the station.

I opened the door to the household altar, revealing the smiling photo of my dad placed there. I straightened up my posture and bowed.

The morning following the ghost-train ride, I returned to my parents' house in Yugawara. After burning some incense in the living room, I headed up the stairs to my father's room. It was my first time setting foot in there since elementary school. I often wrestled with him right here on this tatami matting. I never really pulled out a win against him, but once, right on the cusp of my starting junior high, I managed to pin him underfoot. Looking back, he must have thrown the match on purpose for me.

I noticed a big brown bottle standing in a corner of the wooden home-office desk. I took the bottle out of its holder; it felt heavy in my hands. Judging by the golden label and the *Daiginjo* appellation, it had to be high-end stuff.

"That bottle? Your father bought it when you landed your job."

Mom entered the room.

"Sorry I barged in," I said.

She gently put a hand on the bottle. "He was always telling me how he wanted to drink it with you one day. Just the two of you."

After I got that job from hell, I never returned to my parents' house. I'd been so crazy about Shiho, who I'd just started dating, that I neglected to breathe a single word of thanks to the two people who brought me into this world.

"Mom… I lied. I quit my job," I murmured.

"Tell me something I don't know," she said instantly.

"Wait—how'd you know?"

"How could I not? A new hire up and disappears on them, and you don't think they try calling his parents' house?"

I clammed up, and she dulled her tone.

"Your father told me not to say anything. Said you were doing your level best out there, so we shouldn't say anything. Said if our son falls on his face, he'll get back up again. Said we need to wait until he tells us himself."

I couldn't bring myself to look her in the eyes. Regret and remorse flooded my heart.

"Do you know why he was even on that train to begin with?" she asked, gazing at me with a solemn expression. "Your father—he was on that train to get a new job for you."

"Huh?"

"He was turning to acquaintances for help, going all over bowing his head and asking them to give his son a job. All that, while being dog-tired from working every day. Yet come the weekend, he'd put on a suit he felt so awkward in and start trudging around for you."

"……"

My lips started quivering. A whole mess of feelings clashed inside me, and all of a sudden, things buried in the recesses of my mind started adding up.

At the end of January, money had been deposited into my account under the name of *KRLB*. But I searched for such an institution online, and no Kanto Region Labor Board actually existed. Back then, I'd simply chalked it up to some kind of clerical error, but now it made perfect sense. It was my father who'd sent me that money.

"Food besides just rice got sent to my place; was that Dad, too?" I asked, choking up.

Mom nodded.

I couldn't forgive myself. I'd been such a gutless worm. I felt too low to even stay in the room, so I flew out of there.

Rushing out the front door, I was faced with a small park that held lots of memories. Back in elementary school, there was a summer festival held here. I went to the festival by my lonesome, casting sidelong glances at all the kids having fun with their parents.

As I was sitting on the swing looking lonely, I'd heard someone call out to me from across the road.

"Yuuichi! Yuuichi!"

It was Dad. He'd dropped work to come running so I wouldn't feel so alone.

I rushed up to him, delighted, and jumped into his arms. His work clothes smelled of oil. That odor was so familiar; it signaled to me that Dad was nearby, filling me with relief.

I'd liked that smell. In truth, I'd *liked* the sight of him in his fatigues.

"Sorry I kept ya waiting, Yuuichi. You musta felt so lonely all by yourself."

My father squatted down to be level with me, his eyes watery. He continued apologizing, biting his lip from time to time.

The look on Dad's face when I left the ghost train was the same look he kept giving me during that festival.

His son had saddled him with such a chore when he had work to do, but despite that, my father still thought it was *his* fault. And he'd said his son had quit his job because he, as a father, hadn't listened to me enough. That was just how much he'd loved me.

"AAAAAHHHHHH! AUGHHHHHHHHHHHIIIIIIIIHHHHHH!"

I cried my voice hoarse, falling to my knees on the asphalt, not caring who heard me bawling my eyes out.

A father and his kid were practicing how to ride a bike on a street inside an apartment complex. Since it was Saturday, parents and children were playing all over the grounds.

"Yuuichi! Go carry the bricks in that minitruck over here!"

"Right away, Mr. Takenaka!"

"Don't dawdle now!"

"I'll bring them on the double, sir!"

A meeting hall for the neighborhood association was being constructed in a park built on the premises. I wiped the sweat from my brow with the towel I took from around my neck, rolling up the sleeves of my fatigues. The blocks were heavy, but I'd gained a fair bit of muscle over the past month of manual labor.

The week after riding the ghost train, I moved out of my Tokyo apartment and back to my parents' house in Yugawara. I then asked Mr. Takenaka to give me a job at his construction company.

"Good work today, young man. I made you some nice cold tea. Here."

As I was placing the blocks to the ground, a small old woman appeared with a tray in her hands. She was another tenant at this complex.

"Thanks so much as always, Yuuichi."

"Oh, no, don't mention it."

Ever since we crossed paths, I'd been dropping by her home on a regular basis. Everything Dad used to do for her, I now did. We were casual, chat-over-tea friends.

"Thanks for the tea."

I was about to pick up a glass when I heard a "Sakamoto" from behind. I turned around to find Tagano there.

"What brings you to a place like this, Tagano?"

"I heard through the grapevine the other day that your old man passed away," he said with a meek expression. "Figured since we're peers and all, I should come to your place to burn some incense." He grasped my shoulder. "That must be tough, losing your father."

"How's things going with you and Shiho?" I asked, recounting how I'd seen the two of them at the mall together.

Tagano seemed surprised, but that soon gave way to a wry smile. "She dumped me. She's started going out with some diplomat now. Looks like she's not much for guys who whine."

"...And Mr. Hatakeyama? Is he the same as always?"

"He got promoted. You know what they say—ill weeds grow apace. The way the world's set up, even rat finks like him can reach the heights of power as long as they can do the work. After you left, he started having it out for *me*. He got jealous of my business performance."

Tagano was looking pretty thin. His cheeks were sunken, and his skin looked rough.

"Anyway," he added, "I see you're working for the building contractor your old man used to work at."

"Yeah."

"Having fun at work?"

"I am, actually. It's gonna take some time to get used to it, I think, but I'm always happy to hear customers thank me."

"Huh. I like the look in your eyes, Sakamoto," he said, a forlorn note in his voice. "Well, I've got yet more suits to wine and dine today." Then he did an about-face.

"Tagano," I called as he strode off. He glanced over his shoulder. "Keep at it."

"I intend to," he replied, his expression softening. He waved his hand a little, and then he started walking toward the station.

The entire apartment complex started to take on an orange tinge as the sun went down. That boy who'd been out practicing how to ride a bike was still at it with his father. I was sure he'd succeed in the not too distant future.

I decided to keep working at Dad's company. I was still wet behind the ears as a person, but I wanted to someday surpass my father, who I held in such high esteem. I had the position of company president in my sights. Reason being, I felt surpassing my father would be the number one way to repay his kindness.

And someday, when that ambition came true? I was going to open that bottle of sake in Dad's room.

CHAPTER 3
TO HER, I SAY

The rain was drizzling onto the nursery school's awning, splashing onto the ground and getting my feet all wet.

"Hey, sweetie. Were you a good little boy today?"

A young mother had arrived to pick up the boy taking shelter from the rain next to me. He threw himself at his mother, clinging to her under her umbrella, his expression full of joy. Meanwhile, nobody was coming to pick *me* up. But I'd known that from the start. Because not a soul in this world ever showed me any kindness or affection.

A freezing cold wind shook the gauze on my right cheek. Beneath that was my nasty black birthmark. This disgusting mark had caused me a lot of grief over the years. As the bitter memories cycled through my head, my school bag suddenly started feeling heavier on my back.

On the other side of the street stood a twenty-story high-rise. I was gazing vacantly at the roof of that building, and in search of something that might allow me to hold out hope, I sorted through my memories one more time. Yet hope had been in vanishingly short supply throughout my eleven years on Earth.

My parents divorced when I was in fifth grade after my mom had an affair.

"I'll come see you again, Kazuyuki. I promise."

That was what she'd said before she moved out of our apartment. My dad then took custody of me, but he was a systems engineer who was always busy with work. Every weekday, I spent my time at a local after-school center until Dad got home.

I was small compared with my peers, and that had made me the target of bullying for a long time. I always hid my birthmark with some gauze, but since I'd entered sixth grade, Keigo, another boy in my class, had started making fun of it.

With Dad's hands always being so full, it was commonplace for him to return home late at night. He ended up visiting me at the after-school center less and less over time, forcing me to go home every day by myself when all the other kids had been picked up by their parents.

At school, Keigo's bullying was only escalating.

"'Sup, Marky Mark."

He'd make a crack about my birthmark at any and all opportunities. He'd also stolen my lunch bag, hidden my shoes, and ripped off the gauze on my face in front of my classmates. Our teachers did nothing to help me, and I was left friendless and isolated.

One day, during the third term of the school year, I spotted Mom in the local shopping district. We hadn't seen each other since she moved out, but I figured that as my mother, she'd definitely help me. With this last scrap of hope in my heart, I weaved through the crowd to get closer to her.

"Mom—"

I was rendered speechless. She was cradling a baby, her hand in the hand of a man I didn't know, and she had on the kind of blissful smile she'd never shown in front of Dad.

When our eyes met, she looked surprised, but she soon averted her gaze. She might as well have been telling me that she had no interest in me.

I stood stock-still, and the people behind me pushed past without any consideration. They bumped into my shoulders, but nobody apologized.

I felt utterly unloved and unwanted. And as I watched my mother walk away, I could no longer find a reason to go on living.

The rain had intensified, and there were puddles of black water all over the ground. Kids were getting picked up by their parents one after another, and now the clock was about to strike seven PM. I was the last person under the awning by this point.

I was miserable. It felt like I'd been abandoned, like I was the only one in the entire world. I was scared. The violent downpour was speaking volumes for the frightfulness of the world around me.

It's time I went, I thought. To the roof of that high-rise.

"Hey, kid. You waiting for someone, or…?"

Just as I was about to step out from under the awning, a girl appeared from the other side. She was holding a large umbrella in her right hand, and she bent down to my height. She had on a navy-blue blazer and looked to be around middle school age. Her long, shiny black hair was tied back.

"…"

With those big eyes of hers fixed on me, I couldn't muster any words. The lady was looking at me searchingly as I cast my eyes down out of nervousness. But her gaze wasn't harsh or frightening. When our eyes met, hers softened reassuringly.

Suddenly, a calm and peaceful tune sounded from the nursery-school window. The music box that formed part of the antique clock hanging inside played on the hour. I'd heard this track many times, but I didn't know what it was called.

"Lovely piece, isn't it?"

Her gaze went to the window. She nodded a little to the rhythm of the beat, visibly enjoying the melody that was harmonizing with the sound of the rain.

"Sis!"

The door to the nursery school opened, and a boy with a backpack on came running out. He was usually in the room for the younger kids. I'd never spoken to him, but I saw him around all the time.

"Hi, Yuuta!" the girl said.

"You're late!" Yuuta griped.

"Sorry about that… In any case." Her voice was calm and friendly, and she turned to look at me once again. "Get under my umbrella, kid. We'll go home together."

She gently placed a hand on my head. It was all so sudden, I had no idea what to say.

"Yuuta, I hate to ask, but wait here just a little longer for me, okay? I'll come right back to get you."

"Awww!" Yuuta groaned, disappointed.

"Oh, don't be like that!" she chided, shooting him a pointed look.

"Okay, fine, Takako," he said begrudgingly.

Apparently, her name was Takako.

"All right, kid, let's go."

I didn't reply.

"C'mon already, no need to be shy. This umbrella's waiting for you."

Spurred by the soft smile that wrapped me up, my legs moved on their own. She wasn't tripping the alarm bells all the other strangers did. I stood to her left and gave her a quick nod.

I could tell from the school name written on her blazer and from her lapel badge that she was a middle school third-year. But the way she carried herself was so grown-up that I could hardly believe she was really that young.

She waved at Yuuta as we walked away. "Yuuta, you behave while I'm gone, got it?"

He was sulking, but he still waved back. "See you!"

She took out a yellow handkerchief from the school bag she had over her shoulder. "Here," she said to me. "Wipe your head with this. Otherwise, you'll catch a cold."

"Th-thank you very much…"

My voice was quivering. Up until that point, I'd been bullied constantly, and a stranger had never before been this nice to me.

"So where's your place?" Takako asked.

As I rubbed the back of my head with the handkerchief, I told her.

"Gotcha," she said. "Not too far from mine, then."

We walked side by side through the heavy rain. She had a small plastic bag in her left hand; a sweet smell was wafting from it. She was matching the pace of my short strides in order to keep me under her umbrella and out of the rain.

The nape of her neck looked white as paper, and she exuded elegance and grace from every pore of her body. Whenever our gazes met, I could almost feel myself getting sucked into her dark eyes.

As we passed by Enoura Station, we encountered the large bridge spanning the river. She was about to turn the corner onto the bridge walkway when she quickened her pace. I stepped onto the sidewalk to catch up to her, and before I knew it, she was on my left, having changed which hand was holding the umbrella.

Cars were speeding by us on the bridge, kicking up sprays of water as they went. It was then I realized why she'd switched sides. It must have been to keep me far from the side of the road, just in case I got into an accident.

A potent gust of wind hit my right cheek, lifting the gauze covering my birthmark. My heart started pounding faster. Fearfully, I glanced at her face, but even when she saw my birthmark, her expression remained exactly the same. She smiled and tugged on my left arm. "The wind's getting stronger, so come in a bit closer."

Her uniform was drenched from ceding me so much of the umbrella space, but she didn't complain one bit, unfazed by both the driving rain and the spray of the passing cars.

We crossed the bridge, and after a bit more walking, my apartment complex came into view.

"My place is over there," I told her.

By the time we arrived in front of the building, the rain had diminished into a drizzle. I stepped out from under the umbrella and bowed. "Thank you very much."

She handed me the plastic bag she'd been holding. "They're donuts. Eat them when you get home, if you like."

"Oh, n-no, I can't!"

She pressed the bag against my chest. Still, I tried to decline her generosity, but she squeezed my hands. "Don't feel guilty. Just accept them."

"Thank you...very much..."

"Gotta go. Hang in there, kid."

I watched her walk away until she was out of view. As she turned the corner, she looked at me. She smiled and waved her hand, and I bowed my head deeply.

After getting home, I took the long paper box out of the bag she'd gifted me. There were three brightly colored donuts inside. She'd probably bought them for Yuuta, her kid brother.

While we'd walked together, she hadn't asked me any questions. Not my name, not my age, and not even the circumstances of my home life. Nevertheless, she could clearly tell that I was having a rough time of life. Otherwise, she wouldn't have said, *"Hang in there."*

Alone in the kitchen, I bit into the amber-colored donut. How many years had it been since I got to eat any sugary Western sweets? With each bite, the rich sugar taste spread inside mouth. My throat was feeling weirdly wet—then I realized I was actively crying, the warm tears dripping down my face.

Meeting Takako diminished my desire to die. I still had the yellow handkerchief she'd lent me. I put it in my school bag with the intention of returning it the next time I saw her at the after-school center, but from then on, it was always Yuuta's mother who came to pick him up.

One day in March, I "casually" asked Yuuta about Takako, and he told me that she was working a part-time job even though she was just a middle schooler. According to him, their mother was single, and Takako had to put in hours as a delivery worker after school to help make ends meet.

Apparently, that time Takako had come to pick him up was a rare one-off; it was usually their mother who arrived after she got off work. Ultimately, Takako never visited the after-school center again. When I graduated from elementary school, I also stopped going there.

The blue, blue bay of Sagami filled the horizon beyond the window. I wasn't used to commuting to school by train, but looking out at the ocean from the window brought me some comfort.

"Next stop, Odawarajou-mae. Odawarajou-mae Station."

The doors opened, and a blind woman boarded the train along with her Seeing Eye dog.

"Thank you," she said. "You didn't have to take little old me all the way to the train."

"Don't mention it, ma'am," said the man accompanying her. "This is your first time out with your guide dog; I'm sure you must be anxious."

At that, the woman looked relieved.

That day marked two weeks since I'd started taking this train. I was now attending a municipal middle school near Minami-Kamakura Station. My elementary-school homeroom teacher had told me that people got along with one another better at this particular school. I'd also heard that my tormentor, Keigo, was headed to a more local middle school, and that played no small role in my decision. After consulting with my dad, I chose the municipal middle school, which was about an hour's commute each way by train.

By the time it reached Maekawa Station, things got crowded. When I went to Car Three in search of an empty spot, I saw through the window of the connecting gangway a girl in a school uniform holding a ceiling strap.

I knew that ponytail anywhere. My chest constricted, my heart thumping. It was the girl who'd walked me home that one time. The girl whose face I'd looked up at underneath that umbrella. It was Takako.

She was wearing a white sailor-style school uniform with a bright-red scarf, and she was reading a paperback in her left hand.

The yellow handkerchief was still in my school bag. Though I'd resigned myself to never seeing her again, I carried it with me regardless.

My eyes were glued to the adjacent train car. Every single move I saw her make on that day imprinted in my head vividly and faithfully. We arrived at Minami-Kamakura Station before I knew it, like someone had crunched time into a ball.

I followed her from a distance away as she got off the train. I saw her transfer to a private rail line, so I bought any old ticket. It didn't matter to me if I was late to school. I was too absorbed in following her to care. And then I boarded the same train as her.

She met a female friend on the train and got off at the next station together with her. I followed her through the gates of a large girls' high school on the thoroughfare, about a five-minute walk from the station. Schoolgirls were doing morning softball practice on the sprawling sports field.

I found myself relieved that her school was an all-girls high school. Since the moment I spotted her on the train, I'd been as excited as the time I went to my first-ever summer festival. I didn't follow her because I wanted to thank her for what she'd done for me. Nor was it to return the handkerchief. No—it was because of the huge crush I had on her.

Come the next morning, after I boarded the seven AM rapid train from Enoura Station as usual, I once again spotted Takako in the next car in the exact same place as the day before. She was again reading the small paperback, with a ceiling strap in the other hand.

My excitement at seeing her again had prevented me from catching any sleep. I got such little sleep that I welcomed Dad home when he arrived in the dead of night.

Holding a ceiling strap myself, I observed her from the edge of Car Two. She was facing the side about two meters away from me, the gangway separating our cars. Whenever she looked elsewhere, I quickly pulled back, thinking that she must have noticed me.

Just imagining calling out to her made the back of my neck get sweaty from nerves. My shyness was extreme at the best of times. Confessing to one's crush seemed like such an absurdly tall hurdle to climb that it scared the hell out of me. Of course, it made sense to thank her for that day first and then confess to her at some point in the future. Another way to do it was to become friends and close the distance between us that way before telling her I liked her. Then again, there was no guarantee that she wasn't already taken. She was so pretty that, all-girls school or not, it was still extremely likely that she had a boyfriend. And if she did, was there any point in starting off as friends? And would she even want to be friends with a schlub like me to begin with?

Besides, what if, by calling out to her, nearby classmates started spreading rumors? What if I started getting bullied again because of that? While I didn't have any friends, at least my classmates weren't currently picking on me.

Eating school lunch by myself every day felt lonely, but compared with Keigo's campaign of harassment, I was fine with it.

If I was going to talk to her, it'd be better to do it in some place where no one else was around, just to be safe. And that ruled out this train.

Just as I was musing about that to myself, the train shook, causing her to turn her head my way. Flustered, I found myself crouching down on the spot. A procession of negative thoughts kept me frozen there, unable to move.

It happened the next morning. And the morning after that.

It happened after the Golden Week holidays ended, too.

The bright dawn light was spreading out from the distance like running ink, and the number of suits passing through the ticket gates kept increasing.

I was waiting for Takako near a coffee shop in front of Enoura Station. To be clear—I was lying in wait.

Talking to her on the train was a difficult proposition. Too many pairs of eyes around us. But now, this early in the morning? There weren't many people in front of the station.

I was planning to call out to her and pass it off as a coincidence. For this plan to shine, we had to be coming toward the station from different directions so we could bump into each other by the entrance. That way, our reunion could be a casual affair. Plus, once I met her face-to-face, I wouldn't be able to run away. I was cutting off my escape route.

Starting early the previous week, I'd already been investigating which direction she came to the station from. Incidentally, I'd chosen today because it was ranked the luckiest in the horoscope on that morning's infotainment show. And the fortune was pretty accurate.

I looked at my watch; it was nearly seven. The train departed at seven, so I figured she was about due to come down that shopping area over there. I craned my neck out from behind the coffee shop and spotted her in the distance; she was rounding the corner, ambling down the sidewalk.

She loomed closer, larger, and I hurriedly pulled my head back, despite the fact that she was still quite a ways away. Stress was suddenly assailing me, seeping into me from head to toe. My heart was racing far faster than when I saw her on the train. The blood all throughout my body gathered in my chest, my heart thumping louder and louder.

It'll take her around two more minutes to reach the station. Calm down. Calm down, Kazuyuki.

It's okay.

It'll be okay.

It's not like I'm gonna die. I'm just gonna talk to her, that's all.

But what if I confess and she rejects me? Could I even go on living afterward?

Never mind confessing—today, all I need to do is thank her for last time. That'll put me on the scoreboard. I can do this. I know I can. I can do this!

I jumped out from behind the coffee shop, feigning an air of innocence as I approached her from the side. She'd begun heading for the roundabout after passing through the crosswalk. But the moment I saw her up close, I suddenly veered off. Instead of heading toward the station ticket gate, I proceeded in the direction she'd come from, as if I'd had business to attend to over yonder all along. What was I doing? My legs were moving on their own again. But on the other hand, the wave of relief that washed over me now that I didn't have to tell her how I felt made distancing myself from her feel like a nice comfy blanket.

When I came back to my senses, I found myself in the shopping area far away from the station. My heart quieted down so quickly that I had half a mind to wonder what had gotten me so stressed out earlier. It didn't take long for a terrible self-loathing to set in.

A stray dog walked on unsteady legs out of a back alley, passing me by without so much as looking at me. I felt like the universe was telling me how worthless I was, and it made me want to die.

One day in June, about a month after that day, I was aboard the usual early morning train. Takako's train.

After giving it a lot of thought, I opted for a change in strategy. If I couldn't call out to her myself, I'd just have *her* call out to *me*. After lying in wait in front of the station again, I followed Takako and boarded the same car as her.

In order to get her to notice me, I grabbed a ceiling strap two straps away from her. To my left was an old man reading a weekly paper with a strap in the other hand. He was serving as the wall between us two. Then I waited for her to notice me as I spied her furtively.

I had a small paperback book in my hand. The same one she was reading. Who wouldn't be curious about somebody reading the same title nearby? This book would raise my chances of catching her attention in a big way.

I had found out the title of the book she was reading two days prior, when I peered over from the next car over. She usually covered her books with dust jackets, but not on that day, most likely because it was a library book. Typically, it took her four days to finish a book. She probably read on the train because she was busy with her job and school.

I'd read several other books by that author for the sole reason of being able to reply, *No way, I'm a huge fan, too!* when she called out to me. I didn't forgo after-school club activities for no reason. I was making good use of my time!

But she didn't notice me at all. She was so engrossed in the book that she never looked at me. I affected an unnatural cough. Then I put both hands over my mouth and coughed like I had asthma. But she didn't bat an eye.

Talk about frustrating. I'd brushed my teeth twice that morning, thinking this would be the day we could have a conversation. I'd simulated it in my head so many times. If she asked that question, I had an answer for her. If she asked *that* question, I had an answer for that, too. If she asked me about my hobbies, I'd say I liked to read (because *she* liked to read). If she asked me what I did on my days off, I'd gun for coolness points by replying that I either read books or played some pool. If you're wondering what my actual hobby was, it was watching late-night anime. And on my days off, all I did was veg out at home.

If she said, *By any chance, are you that kid from back then?* my plan was to pretend I didn't recognize her for a few seconds. If I "remembered" her too quickly, it'd be blatantly obvious that I'd been longing to see her again. I had a hunch that if I put on airs just a tiny bit, it'd raise her opinion of me and make all the developments that occurred from that point forward play out to my advantage.

I glanced at her, going over the replies I'd prepared over and over again in my head. But she never noticed me.

"Next stop, Maekawa. Maekawa."

The doors swung open. As I was fretting over how there were only forty minutes left until the train reached Minami-Kamakura, the old man next to me let go of his strap. When I saw him getting off the train, I boldly switched straps over to her. The strapless space in front of the door was the only thing separating us.

There she was. She was *right there*. This was the closest I'd ever come. And that thought got my heart racing.

Calm down. Don't freak out. It's okay. It's not gonna kill you.

Should I try coughing again? If I were to cough at this distance, I was sure she'd look at me at least once. But maybe she'd find it too forced. I mean, I already had the same book as her. Wouldn't it make it super obvious this was all premeditated? If she caught me, she'd basically view me as a stalker, and that would definitely gross her out. Just standing there "reading" was the safer bet. But she wasn't likely to notice me if I only stood still. Little coughs, spaced out believably—that'd serve me better, right?

I was too nervous, too conflicted to actually do anything by the time the train arrived at Koiso Station, where an old hunchbacked woman walked onto the train one step at a time as she minded the gap. A great big crowd of people rushed in from either side of her, unwilling to wait for the slow old woman.

Suddenly, Takako snapped her paperback shut. I hurriedly averted my gaze, but I couldn't help but wonder why she'd done so, so I pivoted my head just a few centimeters to the left and moved my eyeballs all the way to the side so that it wouldn't *look* as though I was staring in that direction. She was finally gazing my way, an earnest and serious expression on her face.

As much as I'd been hoping she'd notice me, my body was stiffening up regardless, and the hand holding the book was starting to tremble. As I peered down at my book, fidgeting restlessly, I sensed her move. She was finally, finally coming to talk to me.

Or so I thought.

"Excuse me, miss, you can come over here if you like."

She passed me by, taking the old woman who was wandering around searching for an empty seat by the hand and guiding her to the priority seating in the back of the car. After helping the woman to her seat, she grabbed the strap behind me and proceeded to continue reading as if nothing had happened.

I no longer had the mental stamina to move to the strap behind me. I made one last desperate attempt by coughing one more time, but no dice.

I tried all sorts of means to get closer to her, starting as soon as the next day.

But each and every scheme ended in failure, because each and every time, the feebleness of my own spirit got in the way. And before I knew it, my freshman year of middle school was coming to an end.

Through the train window, I could view the white sandy beach that stretched out along the coastline. I saw a group having fun playing beach volleyball, as though they simply couldn't wait for the opening of the beach season. When the doors opened at Koiso Station, one of the employees set up a wheelchair ramp.

"I'm so sorry to always be bothering you like this, Mr. Kitamura."

"It's no trouble at all, ma'am. Now, allow me to push you. I'll go nice and slow."

He pushed the wheelchair toward me, beads of sweat on his forehead. His diligence made me feel at ease, which was nice so early in the morning.

I was looking at the next car over me from my usual spot. I was a middle school second-year now, but after all this time, I was still unable to confess my feelings to Takako. The gangway connecting our two cars might as well have been the Berlin Wall. Even though she was two meters away, I just couldn't put my hand on the latch.

"You got your eyes on somebody in that car?"

A man sitting in the long seat in front of me struck up a conversation.

"You've been looking through that door window this whole time."

I looked at his face under lowered brows, and it seemed familiar. Then I remembered. Back when I was new to middle school, he was the one who'd accompanied a woman with a Seeing Eye dog onto the train.

"Forgive me if I'm being rude by asking, but have you got a crush on someone or what?"

"No, I don't!" I replied immediately, as if I'd seen the question coming. *Has this guy got no manners?*

I could sense that I was turning red. Was it that obvious? Embarrassed, I moved from that spot. I supposed it was only natural that the man regarded me with suspicion. In fact, it wouldn't be surprising if somebody straight-up reported a weirdo like me who was peering into the next car over.

The train stopped at Chigasaki Kaigan Station; if one strained their ears by the doors when they were open, they could hear the rolling waves. Whenever I saw that beach while riding this train, I always wished I could be walking it with my hand in hers. Both of us barefoot. Losing track of time as we strolled across the smooth, dry sand. No need for us to say anything. I just wanted to hold hands with her and walk while gazing out on the big blue sea.

But that day never came. Summer rushed by at breakneck speed, and I hadn't been able to fess up or do anything else.

The area in front of Minami-Kamakura Station was bustling with young folks. Every building the eye could see was decorated in hues of red, white, and green. And it felt especially lonesome to hit the town without a companion on the evening of Christmas Eve.

A large, brick café was situated at a point removed from the big boulevard. Ever since the end of November, when I was wandering around Minami-Kamakura after school and happened to see Takako working at that café, I'd been heading there after school and watching her from outside. But today, I was here for a different reason. I wanted to see if she was working on this romantic holiday as opposed to going on a date.

If she did have a boyfriend, it'd be highly unlikely that she'd be at her job this evening. As a young girl, she'd almost definitely be going to some date spot with her boyfriend. Takako usually worked weekdays, which meant that if she wasn't at the café today, the chances were high it was because she had a boyfriend.

I turned from the main avenue onto the same side street as always, and there it was. The familiar storefront. The brown brick roof was adorned with decorative lights featuring Santa Claus and his reindeer.

I approached the café with heavy steps. If she was absent today, it'd spell the end of my long battle. I was torn between wanting to be sure and wanting to remain ignorant. In any case, I wasted no time hiding behind the usual telephone pole.

I thought about what I had been through for the past year and nine months, and it made me scared to look up. But if I knew she didn't have a boyfriend, I could fight another day. I took a deep breath and timidly cast my eyes to the open deck outside the café.

She was there, wearing the gingham checkered shirt she always wore. She had on a Santa hat and was pouring some customers glasses of champagne. I found myself pumping my fists over and over again. I hadn't been this happy since Dad bought me *The Game of Life* when I was in the fourth grade.

Speak of the devil. Dad was there, looking at the shop window next to the café. His company was located in Minami-Kamakura. This was the first time I'd happened upon him. Did he hang around this area all the time? Next to him stood a young woman wearing a fancy fur coat. His girlfriend?

Since about a month ago, Dad had been coming home much later. He placed a thousand-yen bill on the kitchen table every morning to cover dinner for me, along with a note that read, "Sorry to keep doing this to you, Kazuyuki." Dad was doing his best in his own way. Sure, I was lonely, but I didn't mind if he came home late or if he had a girlfriend.

When the café's wall clock struck eight o'clock, Takako, who had changed into her school uniform, exited the place. I followed her from a distance after watching her set foot in a deserted alley.

She came to a stop in front of a church halfway down the street. I hurriedly hid behind a vending machine as the mellow timbre of a pipe organ played from inside the chapel. She gently closed her eyes and basked in the sound. The melody brought back memories of that after-school center I used to go to before middle school. It was the tune that the music box of the antique clock would play on the hour.

On that day of driving rain nearly two years prior, she'd listened to the music-box tune and commented on what a nice track it was. The memories of the two of us walking side by side under her umbrella flashed through my mind vividly.

There was no better time to confess, was there? It was Christmas Eve, after all. The holiday of romance. If it went well, we could even spend our free time together. The knowledge that she didn't have a boyfriend was like a tailwind lifting my spirits. If I was ever going to do it, now was the time.

As usual, my heart began racing. I had to wonder how many times I'd experienced this obnoxious, chest-bursting thumping. But I was still unable to step out from behind the vending machine.

"Yo, sweetcheeks!"

It was then that a pair of young thugs with dyed brown hair approached her from across the street. One placed his hands on her shoulder and brought his face closer to hers. "Whatcha doin' alone on Christmas Eve, cupcake?"

She tried to slip past him, but the hulking hoodlum grabbed her by the wrist. "C'mon, let's go someplace, you and me."

This was bad. This was really, really bad. They looked like dangerous customers; both had piercings, and the larger one even bore a gangster-y tattoo on his right ankle.

Of course, running to help her was certainly one of my options, even against punks like them. If it was for her sake, I was prepared to give my life. But if I revealed myself now, she'd definitely remember who I was. And if that happened, she'd ask what I was doing here, and what explanation could I give her? If, by some chance, she pieced together that I'd been watching her from outside the café every day, she might even see me as a nastier dude than those two.

I found myself shouting before I even realized it. "It's…it's the police! The cops are coming!"

I shifted locations to a place in a nearby side street where the three couldn't see me. "Officer, they're over there! Quick, go save that girl!"

I looked through the gap in the fence surrounding a private house to find that the delinquents had scampered off. What a relief.

"If it ain't you, Kazuyuki. What're you doing in a place like this?"

I turned around. Dad was walking toward me from farther down the road, with the woman from before following him. Too many things were happening at once, and I started to panic. Not knowing what to do, I jumped out onto the street in front of me, covering my face with my school bag as I ran right past Takako.

"Hey! Kazuyuki! Kazuyuki!"

I ran with all my heart. Wheezing and panting, I slipped into the gap between a pachinko parlor and a convenience store.

Was the cat out of the bag? Doubtful—I'd hidden my face completely. I may have been extremely flustered, but I knew I'd have at least had the presence of mind to do a proper job of concealing my identity.

My state of agitation gradually subsided. I proceeded to mentally process what just happened, interpreting it all in a way that was convenient for me and thinking back to ascertain what blunders I may have potentially made.

When I get home and Dad asks me what I was doing, I'll feed him any old answer. What's important is that Takako doesn't have a boyfriend.

The sheer joy of it canceled out any other worries, and a sweet sense of relief filled my chest. But then it suddenly dawned on me. The *real* reason I felt so relieved. It wasn't, in fact, because I found out she didn't have a boyfriend. Nor was it because she'd been unharmed by those two goons. Nor was it because she hadn't caught sight of my face. I was relieved because I got away with not having to tell her how I felt about her. That was the number one reason. I had made zero progress whatsoever, and that was a *comfort* to me. All I'd done was run away. What a pathetic, dyed-in-the-wool coward I was. My own spinelessness astounded me.

Traumatized by that incident, I didn't visit the café again. Even after the coming of the New Year, I wasted my time doing nothing. And so I reached my third and final year of middle school without getting any closer to being able to confess to her.

* * *

When the train doors opened at Maekawa Station, grade-schoolers filed in. At the direction of the teacher accompanying them, they slowly moved toward the back door so as not to bother the other passengers. Were they headed to Kamakura on a field trip? I was envious of all the little kids. They looked so carefree.

Two years had passed since I first spotted Takako on this train. And I still couldn't bring myself to open the gangway door. All I had to do was go to her car and tell her I liked her. I could even get it over and done in ten seconds flat if I played my cards right. And yet for two long years, I just couldn't do it.

The yellow handkerchief she'd lent me on that fateful day was still in my bag. Looking back, I should've returned it to her the first time I saw her. If I had, we might have been able to spend some fun, quality time as friends, even if I never gathered up the nerve to ask her out. But it was too late now. Well, it wasn't actually too late, but to return the handkerchief after all this time? I didn't possess that kind of courage to begin with.

As I brooded about this, that, and the other thing, I cast a glance at the adjacent car. But I instantly averted my gaze. Or rather, I ducked out of the way. Because the apple of my eye with the paperback in hand was staring at me.

This was a first. My head was an endless cloud of question marks.

I slipped into the tight cluster of grade-schoolers. I stealthily craned my neck to ascertain the situation. Her eyes were back on her book. So had that been happenstance? What had that been about?

"You kiddies going on a field trip?" said a man sitting at the end of the long seat.

It was the man who once asked me if I had a crush on someone on the train. I'd seen him riding this train several times since then. He'd most likely caught on to my feelings for her. I didn't want to be on this car anymore, so I checked once again to make sure she wasn't looking at me before exiting.

It happened one day in May.

"Hey, Marky Mark. Been a while, hasn't it?"

I was walking past Enoura Station when someone grabbed my shoulder from behind. I turned to see Keigo there. My sixth-grade bully.

"Still a pip-squeak, I see. Ya haven't grown at all, have ya?"

He'd grown considerably. Now he was about twenty centimeters taller than me—I'd guess at least a hundred and seventy centimeters tall. He was even more intimidating than before, which was saying something.

"Sorry, bud, but mind lendin' me some dough?"

He drew his face, thin eyebrows and all, closer to mine without an ounce of restraint. And going by that look on his ugly mug, he was more than willing to rough me up. I pulled out a thousand-yen bill from my wallet, but he reached in and took all three of the thousand-yen bills.

"Much obliged, Marky. Here, a token o' my gratitude." With a nasty smile, he ripped the gauze from my right cheek. "Yep, gross as ever," he said, guffawing as he ran toward the shopping arcade.

At my middle school, nobody had ever mocked my birthmark. I'd thought I'd shaken free of that complex, but my mood sank after getting ridiculed for the first time in a long while, once again gripped by the low feeling that'd been a constant fixture of my life in elementary school.

Thinking about it calmly and objectively, I realized there was no way confessing to Takako would go okay when I was cursed with a birthmark like this. She'd just get creeped out.

In light of that, what I'd been getting up to for the past two years seemed so incredibly meaningless now. I resolved to stop riding the same train as her. That way, I'd no longer feel the need to confess.

I'd no longer need to confess.

When that thought crossed my mind, I found myself feeling deeply, utterly relieved. The stress that had been dogging my every step disappeared, and the weight on my soul was finally lifted. It felt *refreshing*.

I couldn't possibly fight against that endorphin bomb of relief.

Starting the next day, I took the next earliest train to school instead.

And so she disappeared from my everyday life. That didn't, however, mean that my feelings for her disappeared. While my mental health did improve, it also left me with more time than ever to think about what she was doing.

And whenever I went anyplace, I was always looking for her.

When I was at the station platform waiting for a train, I was looking for her.

When I was at school, I was looking for her.

When I was walking down a side street.

When I was at a convenience store.

When I was in a convenience-store bathroom.

Even when I was outside a convenience store, looking in through the window.

I always felt like I was one with her. Even in places I knew she couldn't logically be, my eyes were on the hunt for her on an unconscious level.

When I saw a woman who looked like her holding hands with a guy or boy in town, my heart damn near stopped. Even trivial little nothings like a similar hairstyle or the same high school uniform had me jumping at shadows, and I invariably followed those people just to make sure they weren't actually Takako by some chance.

"Phew. It's not her…"

Though if she did get a boyfriend, I could finally accept defeat and know peace…

I didn't know what to do anymore.

Another morning, another hour of riding a train that she wasn't on. A ceiling strap in hand, I gazed out at Sagami Bay through the window.

At the end of the long seat sat the man I often saw riding my car. He had a navy-blue backpack at his feet, and he was admiring the scenery outside.

I was lonely and wanted human contact, and suddenly, I found myself wanting to talk to him. This was a man who could see through to my inner self. I felt like I could confide in him about stuff.

"Looks like it'll be the harvest moon tonight."

He turned to look at me, as though he could sense me closing the distance between us. He smiled at me as I stood in front of him.

Seeing that childlike smile put me at ease. "So I hear," I blurted, even though I hadn't, in fact, heard about it.

"That moon sure is beautiful, ain't it?"

"Sure is, uh-huh."

"I'll bet looking at the moon from the Chigasaki coast would be a treat for the eyes."

"Er, if I may, sir…," I started shyly.

He raised the corners of his mouth in a grin: *What is it, kid?*

"I'm sorry—I know it's rude of me, but…do you have a girlfriend?"

What the hell am I doing? Why am I asking him that out of nowhere?

But he didn't look upset or put off. "I do."

"Is romance worth it?"

What had gotten into me? I was being uncharacteristically talkative. But his gentle expression made me feel like I could ask him whatever, and he wouldn't chew me out for it.

"That's a tough question to answer."

"I'm sorry I asked you such a weird question."

"That's okay. Don't worry about it. And yeah, it's a tough question, but my answer's still an unhesitating yes." His expression turned serious. "We're talking about former strangers meeting, holding hands, touching lips, et cetera. I think the birth of that kind of extreme closeness between two people is a wonderful thing. And above all, the fact that, out of the endless sea of people out there, they chose *you*, makes you feel like a million bucks."

"And if they don't choose you?"

"What do you mean?"

"It's just, I was wondering—if you do work up the nerve to confess and they say no, what happens then?" I asked with a strained smile.

"I used to think about it the same way for ages and ages," he replied, shyly scratching his temple. "But ya know what I think? I think you've got a soulmate out there."

"A soulmate."

"You heard me. See, there's a phrase I'm fond of. *Chance encounters.* When people run into each other after long stretches of time. If you ask me, that ain't no coincidence. So if that person's your soulmate, I don't think it can go too poorly in the long run."

The trees in Enoura were starting to turn red. The cold autumn winds were sweeping away fallen leaves along the main street in front of the station. It was at this not-quite-twilight hour that the autumn vibes were especially strong.

I was strolling as I stared into the distance. Then a girl in a white sailor-style uniform approached me from far beyond the railroad crossing. I could tell by the red scarf that she was wearing the same school uniform as Takako.

The girl looked somewhat similar to her, too. But I figured she was probably just another look-alike, as per usual, so I didn't pay the girl any mind. Yet as she loomed larger, my heart rate started going way up. It *was* Takako!

Six months had passed since I last saw her, but it felt like I was beholding her for the first time ever. Even from a distance, I got the vague impression that she was even prettier than before. They said women and girls became more beautiful when they fell in love. Now I was worried—had she fallen for somebody?

Since she was looking at her phone, she didn't notice me. Then the railroad crossing started emitting a harsh, grating noise to the same tempo as her strides; the crossing barrier was slowly coming down before my eyes.

There was another path running parallel to the opposite side of the crossing, which meant there was no guarantee that she'd be continuing straight down. She could very well turn left or right for all I knew.

She put her phone in her jacket pocket. There was no one else around. She walked in my direction, her gaze falling on me.

The words that one man imparted to me ran through my mind.

"But ya know what I think? I think you've got a soulmate out there."

A high-speed train started rushing down the tracks, blocking our view of each other. If, by the time the train was finished going through, she was no longer there, I'd give up on her. If she was there to cross the crossing, then we'd pass each other by at super-close range. Maybe she'd recognize me. Then that'd definitely make her my soulmate. If she was my soulmate, she'd cross. And if she crossed, I'd confess.

The train rushed by, blasting a gust of wind that I felt on my whole body. I looked down at the ground, and then I mustered the determination to stare directly in front of me. My windswept bangs swung back like a pendulum as the last car of the train passed by.

Autumn had given way to winter, and the calendar had shifted to a new year.

"Next stop, Koiso. Koiso."

The doors opened, and passengers flooded in before walking in search of an empty spot. That one man was sitting in the box seat near the gangway connecting this car to Car Three. He was resting his right arm on the edge of the window and looking at the view outside. Our eyes met.

"Long time no see," he said, pointing at the empty seat in front of him with his gaze.

"It's been a while, sir."

"You're on an awfully late train today."

"I overslept. Dozed off while watching a late-night anime marathon." I scratched my head shyly.

He chuckled and smiled. "Last time we met, we talked about romance stuff a bit, didn't we?"

"Yeah, but let's drop that."

My strong tone must have taken him aback; he stared at me searchingly for a while. Then he averted his eyes.

I'd already given up on Takako.

I'd convinced myself that she wasn't my soulmate.

Because she hadn't crossed the crossing that day.

"It's nice how the sea's so big, huh?" he murmured as he looked out the window. "It's strange. Looking out on the big blue ocean, it always makes me feel like I can do anything I set my mind to. The sea never fails to give me courage."

He had a sage look in his eyes. Then those eyes turned toward me.

"Back in high school, there was this girl I liked," he continued with a solemn expression. His gaze returned to the other side of the window, and on occasion, he turned to look at me again, halting and stammering as he spoke. "But I was a shy kid—couldn't bring myself to confess even after it was announced she'd be transferring schools. And after I graduated, I never moved out of the area, because I figured she might one day return to this town. And boy, was that period rough. There was no way she could be around anymore—but I was always on the lookout for her anyway."

Wow, that sounds just like me.

"In retrospect, I was being pretty pathetic. Whenever I saw somebody who looked like her putting her arm in another man's, it scared me half to death. I'd always follow 'em to make sure it wasn't her."

"I know that feeling." I then jumped right to the juicy bit. "What happened with that person in the end?" I spluttered.

"We started dating."

"Huh?"

"More than a decade passed before we stumbled upon each other in town. And now she's my girlfriend."

It was a little gratifying to hear that, as though my *own* efforts had been rewarded.

"When you reunited, were you the one who confessed?"

He smiled wryly. "Yep. Though, I dunno if you could really call it a confession."

"How'd you manage to do it?"

"How? Isn't that obvious?" He gave me a pointed look. "I didn't want any regrets."

I didn't want any regrets.

I didn't want any regrets.

I didn't want any regrets.

His words echoed in my mind.

"I'd been kicking myself for years and years, see. I'd always regretted not telling her how I felt back in high school. I couldn't forgive myself for not doing anything after learning she'd be transferring. So one day, as I stared out at the Kamakura sea, I swore to myself that if I ever bumped into her again, I'd work up the courage to do it."

"……"

What he said was hard for me to hear. His tale of regret pierced my soul.

"Next stop, Chigasaki Kaigan. Chigasaki Kaigan."

The expansive sands of the Chigasaki coast were now in view outside the window.

I'd dreamed of walking down this beach hand in hand with her.

A dream I'd discarded without ever really shooting my shot.

In the box seats next to me, a boy and a girl in school uniforms were touching shoulder to shoulder and holding hands tightly under their seats. The girl was quietly resting her head on the boy's shoulder.

Damn. Must be nice.

The two had carved out a space where nobody else could come near them. My eyes fell on the gangway window I'd peered into thousands of times as I remembered Takako. And as I rued all the time I'd wasted, my heart suddenly started racing.

I couldn't believe my eyes. She was there. Takako was there!

She was holding on to a ceiling strap and reading a small paperback, same as always. What was she doing on the train at this hour? I'd overslept. It was past eleven o'clock already! What kind of miracle was this? Clearly, God was giving me one last chance. No option to chicken out now.

But the calm, coolheaded side of me reared its ugly head. Wouldn't it be better to do it some other time? Shouldn't I try after I brushed my teeth nice and thoroughly? Preparation was key in everything, after all. And if I decided everything I'd say beforehand, it'd raise my chances for sure.

But I shook my head. I was merely looking for a plausible pretext to run away. The same as when I used the birthmark on my cheek as an excuse to write the whole thing off, and the same as when I used the idea that she must not be my soulmate as a reason to avoid being brave and professing my feelings.

"My girlfriend and I are getting married soon," the man from earlier said.

It was already March. A high-school senior like Takako wouldn't be commuting to school much longer.

"She and I became friends in a forest in Odawara, through a dog named Shiro."

There couldn't be many days remaining until her graduation. I was going to be enrolling in a high school closer to home. This was almost certainly the last time I'd ever bump into her on the train.

I…

I don't…

"When we reunited, I told her how I felt. And when we were dating, I proposed to her. I didn't want my time with her…"

I don't want my time with her to end as nothing more than a nice memory.

"…to end as nothing more than a nice memory."

I got to my feet. It was time to take a bulldozer to the Berlin Wall. Why let fate decide when I could take fate in my own hands?

I pulled the gangway door open and set foot in Car Three, closing the distance between us.

"Er, excuse me," I said.

She shut her book and turned to look at me.

But just before our eyes could meet, the train derailed.

Inky blackness stretched as far as I could see. Was I looking at the black from outside it or from inside it? I couldn't tell. All I could sense was the vast expanse of pitch darkness, and I felt weightless and floaty. From time to time within the darkness, something flickered into view, not unlike a dream where the scene or place kept changing.

I saw the train car tumbling.

I saw blood pouring from people's heads as they collapsed.

I saw a steep cliff over a gorge.

It was a peculiar sensation. It felt like those visions were blending together in a loop without end.

And then somebody suddenly picked me up.

"Kazuyuki!"

Someone was calling my name, I think.

Before long, I found myself in front of a wall of pure white. Eventually, I realized my eyes were blinking. And I was dimly aware of where I was, and that the white "wall" was, in fact, the ceiling.

"Doctor, Kazuyuki is awake!"

A woman wearing a white coat ran out of the room. The EKG next to my bed and the smell of disinfectant pervading the room told me where I must've been.

"You're at Minami-Kamakura General Hospital. You were in a train accident."

The elderly doctor who appeared launched into a lengthy explanation while holding a stethoscope to my chest. I wasn't too seriously injured in the accident, getting off with three broken ribs. It was March 26; apparently, I'd been out cold in this hospital for around three weeks.

What the doctor was telling me wasn't clicking in my head. I had no recollection of the accident, and my memories leading up to the accident were fuzzy at best.

That evening, Dad came to visit me in my hospital room. I remembered him clearly. He called out to me with worry in his voice, but he frequently left the room with his phone in hand. Work, most likely.

A young woman came into the hospital room in Dad's stead. She had on a ton of makeup, and her perfume was extremely potent.

"My name's Chiaki, and I'm dating your father." She peeled me an apple by my bed.

I once saw her with Dad in town near that café. For some reason or other, I got the feeling he'd be marrying her soon.

The next day, a police officer began visiting me. He asked me a truckload of questions about the derailment, but I was no help; I still couldn't remember anything.

Then something happened five days after coming to. I noticed my school bag leaning against the corner of the room. Shrugging off the pain in my ribs, I got out of bed and picked it up. Opening it, I spotted the yellow handkerchief inside. I'd put it in a zipped-up plastic bag, so it had to be important to me.

As I looked at the handkerchief in my hand, my heart skipped a beat. Distinct and discrete memories of her surged inside my head like an avalanche. I could feel how much I was sweating on the back of my neck. The memory fragments were linking into place at a rapid pace, as if somebody had unplugged the drain and all the floating shards were getting sucked together into one big ball.

"Taka…ko…"

We'd both been on that train that day. And I'd been about to tell her how I felt, but the moment I stood next to her, the train rocked violently. Was she okay? What was she doing now? I couldn't just stay in my room without knowing, so I put on a jacket that was on a hanger in my room, changed into a pair of jeans, and dashed out the door.

"Where are you going, young man?!"

I pulled away from the nurses and bolted out of the building. For all I knew, Takako was somewhere in this hospital, but for the time being, I had one destination in mind. Because if I made it there, I'd probably find out what happened to her.

Since the Kamakura Line was suspended, I took a roundabout route to Enoura via Tokyo. Under the dusky skies, I headed to the after-school center as fast as my legs could carry me.

"Yuuta!"

Yuuta was looking lonely sitting on a bench in the park behind the center. When he noticed me, he stood up; he was a little taller than he'd been three years ago.

"Do you remember me, Yuuta? Remember how I used to come here, too?"

He nodded.

"Your sister was in the recent train derailment, right?" I asked, voice cracking. "What happened to her? Is she doing okay?"

A pause. "She's dead."

"What—?"

"My sister's dead. She died in the train crash!"

"……"

Tunnel vision. I saw nothing but Yuuta's face anymore. Everything else had vanished from my sight.

"You're joking…"

I was shaking him by the shoulders, but however much I couldn't believe it, the tears that began pouring from his eyes told no lies.

Yuuta explained to me in detail what had happened in the accident, sniffling and sobbing all the while. Takako had apparently died in the train car as it fell off that cliff.

"She was all set to start attending nursing school this spring."

Takako had lost her father to illness when she was in elementary school. She wanted to become a nurse in order to save people's lives. And to earn enough money to cover tuition, she worked constantly during all three years of high school.

I just stood there, unable to reply with so much as an *uh-huh* to anything he said. I was in a daze, rooted to the spot.

I was discharged from the hospital at the end of April after my rib fractures healed.

Once I got to high school, my classmates regarded me, the train-derailment survivor, with utmost curiosity. And since I'd started going to school later than everybody else, I was unable to fit in with the rest of my peers.

"Hey there, Marky. You got the luck of the devil, don'cha?"

Someone came from the back of the classroom and tore the gauze off my right cheek.

"Don't hide your birthmark, silly. Let it show loud and proud."

It was Keigo. Not only did he go to my high school, but we were even in the same class. He still had his hair dyed brown.

"I'll be takin' my pocket money, thanks," he said, patting me on the head.

That marked a turning point—afterward, I became isolated in my class.

And really, what reason did I have to go on living anymore?

The steep valley was gaping wide, a stream flowing across its faraway floor.

The train car lying on a riverbank was covered with a blue tarpaulin, as if a giant had gift wrapped a toy train.

I visited the cliff where Takako died, looking for something—anything— to hold on to. It took about a half hour from Minami-Kamakura Station to get to this cliff by foot. More than a few bouquets had been placed along the cliff.

The fencing on the cliff's edge had been savagely dented, speaking volumes as to the sheer force of the impact. The part of the fence that had been completely torn off must have been where the train crashed into it.

I had my hands together in prayer on the roadside when a young woman came up the slope with a large bouquet in hand. She bent down next to me and clapped her hands together.

"…Who did you lose?" she asked me before she gently got to her feet. "My name's Tomoko Higuchi. I lost my fiancé in the crash. My beloved."

She went into her story. Apparently, she was currently pregnant.

"…I lost the girl I love," I said.

Her sincerity made me open up. I told her how I'd crushed on Takako from afar for years, and how, just as I'd mustered the courage to confess, the train derailed.

Ms. Higuchi didn't make fun of me for my awkward and bungling life thus far. Instead, she smiled softly, like a mother would to her child; she listened to my story, nodding repeatedly with understanding.

"If you could see that girl one more time, would you do it?" she asked me.

According to her, if I visited Nishi-Yuigahama Station late at night, I could see a ghost girl named Yukiho as well as the phantasmal train that sped down the Kamakura Line tracks during the wee hours of the morning. And if I so wished, I could take a ride on that train on the day of the disaster.

Judging by the look on her face, Ms. Higuchi wasn't yanking my chain. I could sense that she'd told me this out of genuine sympathy. I was sure I could trust this lady. And more than anything, I'd jump at any chance to talk to Takako. I wanted to tell her how I felt at any cost.

"I think you should see her again."

That strong sense of purpose in Ms. Higuchi's eyes made me long for Takako even more. I resolved to meet this Yukiho that night.

The moon-drenched platform was so silent, I could have sworn I was in the depths of the sea. I could even hear the faint ticking of the platform clock's minute hand.

The *thud, thud, thud* of footsteps echoed from deep inside the platform, punctuating the quiet of the wee hours. A tall girl in a sailor-style school uniform stopped in front of me.

"...Are you Yukiho, miss?" I asked.

"Yep," she replied brusquely, her lips curling a tiny bit. "A pleasure. Hope you don't mind I'm a ghost."

When Ms. Higuchi told me this girl was a ghost, I'd expected some hair-raising specter, but she didn't look any different from a normal person. Her body wasn't transparent, either, for that matter. In any case, I summarized my history with Takako for her.

"So you were on the train when it crashed? Well, you're a rare case."

"Is it true? Is there really a ghost train?" I asked, cutting to the chase.

She flashed a toothy grin. "Heh-heh. Impatient, aren't we? Oh, it's true, all right."

Then she pointed her chin in the direction of the translucent train that was slowing to a stop by our platform.

My heart raced from astonishment. I could see a whole load of passengers on the train, and I could hear their voices as they spoke, just as anybody on the platform would normally hear when the train was there.

Yukiho folded her arms. "This train is the very same train that crashed on that day." Her tone made it clear she'd said this a million times.

Apparently, the ghost train was visible only to people with strong feelings regarding the accident, and if I boarded it, I'd be able to see victims who died once again—corroborating what Ms. Higuchi had told me.

After hearing Yukiho's primer, I tried to ask her the questions that sprang to mind—but she'd obviously anticipated that, because she immediately added, "However..."

- You may board the train only from the station where the doomed rider first boarded.
- You mustn't tell the doomed rider that they are soon to die.
- You must get off the train at or before passing Nishi-Yuigahama Station. Otherwise, you, too, shall die in the accident.
- Meeting the doomed rider will not change their fate. No matter what you do, those who died in the accident will not come back to life. If you attempt to get people off the train before it derails, you will be returned to the present day.

As I stood there, processing all that, a violent *crash* thundered from the direction of Minami-Kamakura Station. Yukiho looked down the tracks. "If you don't get off at or before passing Nishi-Yuigahama Station, you'll join the dead. Oh, and the ghost train's presence is thinning more and more. One day, it'll ascend into the sky, so if there's someone you wanna see, go and see them. If you head to the station where your person boarded the doomed train, then that train will come. Bye now."

She raised her hand in farewell before disappearing.

Silence descended upon the pitch-dark platform once again. I stood by the tactile paving and stared in the direction the train had passed. Takako had been on that train, and that was enough to make me stare off into the distance for ages.

I had no second thoughts.

The entire platform was shrouded in deep-black darkness, and the moon was radiating its faint and cold light through the gaps in the cloud cover. When I went to check my watch, sunlight began to melt the darkness; now what surrounded me was the view of Enoura Station that I'd seen on the morning of the accident.

A semitransparent train approached from Yugawara's direction. Just as the train pulled into the platform, Takako half ran through the ticket gate. She slipped right into Car Three and heaved a sigh of relief at making it in time. I boarded Car Two, just as I had done before. It would take less than fifty minutes for the train to reach Nishi-Yuigahama Station. I didn't have a single second to waste—but there was something I had to do before I could go up to her.

After a while, the train stopped at Odawarajou-mae Station. When the door opened, a man carrying a navy-blue backpack got on board. From a little distance away, I saw him sitting down on the box seat by the window.

I let out a deep sigh. I'd been hoping against hope that he wouldn't get on the train, even though I knew it was pointless. Last night, I'd seen that same man aboard the ghost train when it appeared at Nishi-Yuigahama Station. This meant that after we'd had that chat on the day of the accident, he'd died in the crash. Otherwise, he wouldn't be here.

"…Good morning, sir," I said.

"Hiya," he replied, raising a hand in greeting.

I dipped my head slightly, and then my expression stiffened as I bowed deeply at the waist. "Thank you so much for listening to everything I had to say."

I knew thanking him this emphatically would come across as strange; in this timeline, we'd never talked to each other. But even if that made him think I was a weirdo, I just had to express my gratitude. If it wasn't for him, I never would've acted on my feelings. He was the one who'd given me the push I needed.

"…Now I'm going to go tell the girl I like how I feel," I told him.

He got to his feet, and without questioning anything, he proffered his right hand. I gripped it tight. Naturally, the man had no idea he'd be dying in an accident later, and yet his grip was so strong, it was as though he was entrusting me with something.

"Don't want it to be nothing more than a nice memory, see," I added.

To that, he grinned. Then he let go of my hand at last, albeit reluctantly, and sat back down to resume gazing at the sea.

All worked up now, I placed my hand on the gangway door. I was wearing my old middle school uniform. I'd watched her while wearing this uniform throughout the three years I spent there. This felt right; there was no other set of clothing I could possibly wear when I confessed to her.

I stepped into Car Three and spotted her facing off to the side. Just like on that day, she was holding on to a ceiling strap and reading that paperback. With her right before my eyes, a small kernel of hesitation sprouted within me, but an emotion strong enough to bury that hesitation crested slowly from deep within me. I strode forward and came to a stop next to her.

"Er, excuse me." My quivering voice belied my act of bravery.

She closed her book and turned to look at me. Our eyes met; we were less than fifty centimeters away from each other.

This was the first time I'd looked her right in the face since that rainy day all those years ago. And now that the apple of my eye was up close, my vocal cords constricted, refusing to cooperate.

Yet her gaze was gentle and kind. Maybe she'd realized how nervous I was, because she smiled reassuringly.

"Get under my umbrella, kid. We'll go home together."

Her expression now was the same as when she'd started talking to me on the day we first crossed paths. Her soft smile was a warm, encompassing blanket.

"Er, uh, I—I, uh..."

"I remember you. You're the kid I walked home that one time, right?"

A pause. "You... You remembered me."

She nodded, still smiling. Her eyes looked just as big and beautiful as they had back then. But as she stared fixedly at my face, those eyes started swimming.

"Wh-what's the matter?" I asked.

"Oh, uh, no... Never mind... It's nothing." She wiped away her tears. "You going to school?" she said, trying to change the subject.

"Yeah. I overslept a bit today," I admitted, embarrassed.

She covered her mouth and chuckled. "Actually, I overslept, too! Today's the rehearsal for my graduation ceremony, but there was this anime marathon on TV late last night that I really liked, and I ended up watching till early in the morning."

"Me too!" I said, smiling.

"You're kidding! You too?!" Her eyes lit up.

We lost track of time as we enthusiastically discussed our favorite anime, holding on to our respective ceiling straps all the while.

"Apart from anime," she said, "I'm also big into books."

"Me too!"

I'd read the same books I saw her read in the next car over, dreaming of this conversation taking place. It felt like my hard work was paying off now, and I was delighted.

I was having fun. A lot of fun. In fact, this exact moment in time was the most fun I'd ever had in my entire life.

The whole time I was with her, I was a ball of nervous energy, but not in the don't-slip-up-or-she'll-hate-you way. As we conversed, I stopped to think back on every sentence I uttered, combing for anything problematic, but that felt nice somehow. Even binding myself that way felt blissful when I was with her.

However, my eye caught the changing scenery outside; we were approaching the end of the line, and a black shadow gripped my heart. My minutes in heaven would soon come to a close. In less than half an hour, Takako would meet her fate, and that was the immutable reality of things.

The more I came to adore her, the more painful parting with her would become. And when that stark fact dawned on me, I clammed up, unable to look her in the eyes any longer.

Outside the window, the vista of the Chigasaki coast was now coming into view.

"Gorgeous, isn't it? That coastline." She cast her gaze outside, looking a tad forlorn now.

The deep-blue sea was striking, vast. And it contrasted beautifully against the pale-white sand.

Over the past three years, no matter what train cars we were in, we'd looked out at the same scenery every morning. And I'd daydreamed about walking that beach hand in hand with her. Staring as the waves broke to a steady rhythm, the drawers of my memory opened one by one.

I recalled the time I waited for her in front of the station. The time I gripped that ceiling strap while riding the same car as her, so close yet so far. The times I watched her from outside her café. The Christmas Eve I ran away while hiding my face from her. The times I followed someone who looked like her. The time I bumped into her at that railroad crossing. And of course, the time I walked under her umbrella…

And as the curtain began to fall over my long and lonely battle, part of me wondered whether I should even tell her how I felt anymore. But the big blue ocean I was gazing at spurred me to speak.

"You, uh… You saved my life."

She said nothing. I let go of the strap and stared straight at her.

"On the day you walked me home under your umbrella, I was planning to die. I don't have any friends to speak of. My parents are divorced, and my dad's too busy to really look after me. Also, I have this really big birthmark on my right cheek that I keep hidden with this gauze here. I'm tiny for my age, and I've been bullied a ton as a result. But that one day, you let me under your umbrella. And I've never forgotten how sweet the donuts you so graciously gave me were. It was like you were telling me it's okay to go on living… I still have the donut box, too. I kept it. That's all to say…I owe you my life."

I continued, never taking my eyes off her.

"Over the three years since then, I've been watching you from afar. Every morning, I watched you from the next train car over. But I wasn't brave enough to come talk to you. And whenever I happened to see you in town, I could never work up the courage. I just went home. So I… I, uh…"

A moment's hesitation had me looking at the floor again, but then I held my head up and said the words.

"…I like you."

She didn't respond.

"I love you more than anybody in the world. Now and forever."

"……"

"I can never stop thanking my lucky stars…" I screwed up the last of my willpower and looked at her with intensity. "…that our paths crossed."

"………"

And I kept my eyes on her for a while afterward. The passengers around us were staring at us now, wondering what this was all about. She stayed silent for a moment, a sober look on her face, before heaving a slight sigh.

"Thank you," she said wearily. "Thank you…"

And then tears started trickling down her cheeks.

"Huh? Why am I crying? Maybe it's because I've never had a guy tell me he likes me before…" She spoke rapid-fire to draw attention away from her crying, then quickly wiped the tears from her eyes. "Or maybe it's because you're such a great guy."

"……"

I felt my face flushing. Abashed, I blinked rapidly. Seeing her eyes were still teary, I took the yellow handkerchief out of the bag I had slung across my body. I held it out to her.

"This is the handkerchief you lent me that day."

She pushed it back. "I want you to hold on to it. And I want you to think of it as a genuine token of how I feel. Because as of now, I've fallen for you. Let me say that again. I like you, Kazuyuki."

"………"

A big mental eraser rubbed out any and all brain activity I had. It was so confusingly sudden that I cast my eyes down, as if to run from everything in existence. Gradually, I grew more and more teary-eyed myself. I slowly looked up again, and when she flashed me a smile, my gaze flew toward the window.

Facing the wide expanse of sandy beach, I grasped her left hand. Her cheeks turned red, but she squeezed me back. We held hands the whole time as we looked out on the Chigasaki coast. The sun was shining on waves of blue, and flecks of light played on the glittering surface.

The day after, I headed to the cliff where Takako died and laid a rose bouquet on the side of the road. What had happened the night before fresh in my mind, I squatted down and clapped my hands in prayer.

I was here to follow her into the next world. In a drawer in my room was the suicide note I'd written earlier that morning. If I was going to die, I wanted to die in the same place she had.

Something happened when I stood back up in order to jump over the fencing and off the cliff.

"Forgive me if I'm overstepping, but if I may ask—did you lose someone in the train crash?"

A middle-aged man who'd been gazing at the valley by the roadside came up to me.

This guy's getting in the way, I thought as I replied, "I did."

"I see. I'm really sorry. That was a rude question." He bowed his head courteously. "I was actually on the train when it derailed, too."

"...Oh, wow. Huh."

"It was a devastating crash, but I lucked out. My injuries were minor... By the way, I saw a girl do something unbelievably heroic on that train," he added with a sincere and earnest look on his face. "I was in Car Three when it happened. The moment the derailed train car seemed about to fall off the cliff, I was fortunate enough to have been flung outside the car. I reached for a young girl who was still inside, but she asked me to pull out a young boy before her!"

I said nothing.

"She must've been a high schooler, judging by her uniform, but she lifted a smaller kid up into my arms as the car was beginning to slip off the cliff. And it fell down right after."

Something like a premonition coursed through my body as I listened to his account.

"Could you describe him to me? Please tell me what you know! What boy did that girl save?" I begged.

"I was injured, too, and it was so chaotic that I don't really remember what he looked like, but...I do remember he had a large birthmark on his right cheek."

My heart was pounding now. My breath caught in my throat; the thumping in my chest was like a broken metronome. Suddenly, my head was spinning.

Shards and fragments of memories flowed into my brain without context or coherence. It was akin to a real-life flashback, this sensation. I'd encountered it before around when I'd been unconscious in the hospital.

The interior of the train car as it tumbled. The passengers with bleeding head wounds. The sight of the steep cliff over the ravine. They all blended together, until eventually, somebody lifted me up. And the image of who that person was rose to the surface, clear as could be in my mind.

She was the girl I regarded as the most precious person to me in all the world. And she'd shouted:

"Save him first! Please! Save Kazuyuki first!"

I was so shocked, flabbergasted. But at the same time, I felt something was *off* about the words that reverberated inside my head. What she'd told me on the ghost train echoed in my ears.

"Because as of now, I've fallen for you. Let me say that again. I like you, Kazuyuki."

It was weird. I'd never once told her my name. Back on that rainy day, she'd never asked me my name, so I didn't introduce myself. I remembered what we'd said that day like it was yesterday, so I was dead certain. Nor had she asked me my name on the ghost train. She should've had no way of knowing.

I reeled in more memories from the recesses of my mind, and in the process, one thing struck me as pertinent. During Christmas Eve of the year prior, when I ran away while hiding my face using my bag, Dad had shouted *"Kazuyuki!"* more than once. There was only one plausible explanation—Takako must have noticed me then. She must have realized that the kid who'd run away holding a bag over his face was the elementary schooler she'd walked home on that rainy day. And she *had* looked directly at me, that one time on the train. It made sense if she realized I'd been watching her on the train after Christmas Eve.

She'd saved me during the crash, *knowing* who I was. She'd saved my life a second time. My conjecture was swiftly becoming conviction. Emotionally overwhelmed, I was at a loss for words. I fell to my knees, the cold wind whistling in my ears.

*   *   *

Amid the gloomy darkness, the rain continued without pause. And the more I walked, the heavier my umbrella felt under the pounding precipitation.

Little Yuuta was under the awning of the after-school center with his back-pack on.

"Hey," I said as I came closer, bending at the waist to stoop level to him. "Is anyone coming to pick you up, Yuuta?"

He shook his head dejectedly.

"Where's your mother?"

"Mommy's been busy with work ever since Takako died."

"…I see. All right. In that case, get under my umbrella. We'll go home together," I said, softening my expression. "I could never replace your sister. But what I can do is, at the very least, come pick you up. Starting today, I'll be the one to do just that."

A tiny smile appeared on his face. "Thanks, mister," he said bashfully before coming under my umbrella.

His hair was wet and looked glossy from the rain. I stopped, taking the handkerchief out of my school bag and wiping his hair. It was the yellow handkerchief Takako gave me. The one she told me to hold on to forever.

"Yo, Marky!"

Just as we were about to leave, Keigo stepped in front of us to block our way.

"You didn't go in the usual direction after leavin' school, so I thought I'd follow ya. Whatcha doin' in a place like this?"

"C'mon, Yuuta, let's go."

Keigo yanked me by the arm. "Bad move, tryin' to ignore me," he said, eyes angry under his umbrella. "Whatever. Just gimme my money."

A brief pause. "No."

"What'd you say to me?" I shook him off, and he had a different look on his face now. "What's with the attitude you've been givin' me?! Hey! I'm talkin' here!" he shouted, shoving me in the chest.

"Stop it!" cried Yuuta, who tugged at Keigo's sleeve.

Keigo knocked him down. "Stay outta this, ya little punk!"

"What're you doing?!" I shouted, stooping down to Yuuta where he lay face up on the ground. "You okay, Yuuta?"

"Don't get all cocky, Marky. Look at you, usin' that filthy, tattered-ass handkerchief."

"What did you just say?"

A wild, violent wrath seethed from deep within me. I tossed aside my umbrella and glared at him.

"The hell? What's with that look?" he spat.

"Take it back."

"Excuse me?"

"TAKE BACK WHAT YOU SAID!"

"You're outta your damn mind!"

He smacked my right hand, and the yellow handkerchief fell to the ground.

"Cut it out already!" he yelled.

I couldn't keep it in anymore. I sent a punch his way, but my fist swished through the air. He grabbed me by the wrist and landed a kick.

"Real gutsy all of a sudden, aren't ya?! Take that! And that!"

He kept kicking me in the abdomen from the side. Even as I moaned in pain, I wrapped my arms around his right leg before it could hit me and twisted it down.

"Apologize! Tell Takako you're sorry!" I yelled.

He got up and kicked me on the side before taking my wallet from my pocket. Then he turned around and made to leave, only for me to cling to him from behind.

"You don't know when to quit, do ya?!"

"I refuse to give in to you! 'Cause if I ever did, I'd never be able to look Takako in the face again!"

"The hell are you even talking about?!"

"Tell me—have you ever loved anybody for real in your life?"

"What'd you just say?!"

"I *said*, have you ever loved anybody?!"

"Of course I haven't, dumbass!"

"Yeah, that's what I thought. And that's why you're *weak*. Way too weak to ever get the best of me!"

I lifted him off the ground from behind and threw him down. As we got tangled up in the soaking rain, Yuuta leaned above us.

"Don't pick on my friend!" he shouted.

Little Yuuta began laying into Keigo's abdomen, but Keigo got up and started kicking us both.

"Hey, what's going on over there?!"

One of the after-school center's employees noticed the commotion and rushed over, umbrella in hand. Keigo clicked his tongue and made to leave, but I wrapped my arms around his waist from behind once again.

"Quit it already, dumbass!" he hollered.

"Apologize! Tell Takako you're sorry! Go on, say it! Tell her! *Say you're sorry!*"

I bit his right hand.

"Owww!"

I sank my teeth deeper still.

Not to be outdone, Yuuta bit his other hand.

"Ow! Owww!" Keigo hollered.

"I'll keep on biting if you don't apologize! So say…you're…*sorry!*" I demanded.

"Ow! Ow, ow, ow! Okay, I'm sorry!"

"And gimme my wallet back! Leave it right there! Leave it!"

"*Owww!* Okay, fine, okay! Sorry! I'm sorry! Ow! *Ow!*"

I stopped biting, and then so did Yuuta, who looked thoroughly pleased with himself. Keigo ran from the employee who'd appeared.

"What happened?!" she asked us.

As I panted, I told her it was nothing more than a tiff with a friend. She wasn't terribly convinced.

"Starting today," said Yuuta, "I'm gonna go home with *him*. 'Cause he's like a real big brother to me."

That was such a resolute and undaunted statement coming from a grade-schooler. The employee must have seen how determined he was.

"All right. Take care now, you hear?"

And with that, she returned inside.

"You okay, Kazuyuki?"

"Yeah, I'm fine," I said, plucking the handkerchief off the ground. "You hurt anywhere, Yuuta?"

He shook his head, purpose in his eyes. In his dignified expression, I saw flashes of Takako. I picked up the umbrella, and he came over next to me.

"I'm so wet that going under the umbrella won't do anything for me," he said, grinning.

Through the sound of the rain, I heard a familiar melody play from inside the building.

"Oh, hey, that's that track Takako liked," I noted.

Yuuta's gaze went toward the playroom. The music box attached to the wall clock was announcing via the sweet melody that it was seven PM.

"She's told me before," Yuuta said. "About how this track is her favorite in the whole world."

"...What's it called?"

"It's called 'Hymne à l'amour.'"

The high-pitched tinkle of the music box permeated my eardrums, the relaxing melody coursing through my entire body as if to convey something to me. My eyes were turning moist as I just barely managed to hold back the tears from spilling over.

I need to be stronger...

But it was no use. The tears soon became twin streams running down my cheeks.

I wiped my eyes using the already-drenched handkerchief. Then I heaved a deep sigh, determined to move forward, and I looked straight ahead with a fire in my eyes.

"All right, Yuuta. Let's go, shall we?"

I peeled off the gauze on my right cheek.

CHAPTER 4
TO DAD, I SAY

The love of my life finished using the shoehorn and handed it over.

"Have a good day, Dad," I said from the hallway.

"Thanks. See you later."

The tall man looked over his shoulder at me, averting his gaze slightly—the same this morning as many others. He was a shy man who didn't talk much. Even though we were husband and wife, he still never looked me in the eye in the morning when he said his "See you later." He was so diffident that part of him still felt abashed about our relationship.

As he closed the front door, he looked at me for a split second through the gap that it left. When our gazes met, his eyes lit up a bit before he closed the door all the way. For whatever reason, it always felt like in that moment, when we looked each other in the eyes, we were bearing our hearts to the other, and I secretly anticipated it every morning.

Hana, who'd been curled up asleep in the rocking chair in the living room, opened her big eyes wide. She meowed as she clambered up the open window and slipped outside.

Peeking through the front door, I saw Hana hanging around my husband's legs, her gray fur swaying as she fidgeted. It was as if she was apologizing: *Sorry I was so late to see you off.*

He bent down and picked her up, gently patting her head.

"All right, Hana, I'm off. See you later," he said, his expression softer now. *This is what they call marital bliss, isn't it?* I found myself thinking. I half-seriously considered whether there might be a way to cordon off this space and preserve this precious moment in time.

This ordinary scene from our ordinary lives was supposed to repeat itself tomorrow and the next day. But that wasn't to be. Because that morning was the last time I'd see my husband alive.

About six hours had passed since I saw him off at the door. After eating some lunch in the kitchen, I went to the living room to give Hana a snack. She was curled up in her rocking chair.

I turned on the TV while handing Hana some jerky. They were making a heck of a fuss on my screen. A train was lying on its side on the tracks.

"It looks as though the death toll is already in excess of twenty," a reporter announced into a microphone in front of the station.

It was the Touhin Railway. The Kamakura Line. The rapid train that had departed from Nishi-Yugawara Station at 10:26 AM.

As the information trickled in, I quickly grew nervous. That was the very same train my husband usually manned, and he was supposed to be on the clock until the evening. There were other conductors, of course, but considering the time he'd left home this morning, it was more than possible that he'd been in the accident.

Panicking, I called the train company, but I couldn't get through. No matter how many times I called, the line was always busy.

"This just in. It seems Car Three of the six-car train is about to tumble over the cliff."

The more new information the TV beamed into my house, the more my body started trembling. I took out my smartphone, intent on calling up the office one more time, but my fingers were shaking too much to press the screen.

I believed in my husband. He'd worked for Touhin Railway for nearly forty years, and not once had he missed a day of work or come in late. He'd been a train conductor since before we got married, and he'd never committed any noteworthy mistakes. Sure, he was three years away from his sixtieth year on this Earth, but he wasn't senile enough to be making mistakes at the wheel. As his wife, I could declare that for a fact.

Hana sidled up to my legs as if I was her anchor in this world, and I picked her up. *Please watch over your papa, Hana*, I thought as I hugged her.

A young presenter on the screen raised her voice. *"We have some fresh new information coming in. It seems the conductor has probably already died. I repeat, the conductor is likely already—"*

I found myself turning off the TV's main power supply. Before I knew it, Hana was back on the floor.

At that moment, my landline phone lit up. My body twitched like from a Pavlovian reflex. It was unusual for my home phone to ring at this hour. A foreboding feeling glooped over me like syrup. I was too scared to pick it up. Part of me expected the phone to stop bullying me if I just stood there, but no matter how long I waited, the ringing continued.

"Hello?"

"I'm very sorry for taking up your valuable time. I'm with Touhin Railway and—"

As soon as I heard the words *Touhin Railway*, my vision started swimming. I knew what they were going to say before they even said it. It felt like I was listening to this person speak from afar. The only information that stuck was that they were from Touhin. Every other word only reached my brain after a delay.

When I put the phone back, I collapsed on the spot. The call had informed me that my husband was no longer with us.

His body was quietly cremated at a small local funeral home. As a member of the family of the man who'd caused the derailment, I could hardly hold a funeral for him in public. We had no children, and both my parents and his had already passed away. The few remaining relatives we had saw him off to the other world away from the public eye.

My life changed completely after the disaster. Like a once-clear sky suddenly wrapped in darkness.

*   *   *

"…Yes, hello?"

"Ah, hello. Have I reached the home of the killer conductor?"

I hung up the phone before returning to the chair in my living room, putting a hand to my forehead and heaving a heavy sigh. The thumping in my chest showed no sign of calming down any time soon. About a week had passed since the accident, and I'd started to receive prank calls on my landline:

"Drop dead, scum."

"You're just as guilty as he is."

"How long do you plan to go on living like nothing happened?"

I was being subjected to unrelenting verbal abuse day in and day out, with no time for my heart rate to recover. The layers of generalized anxiety I'd been feeling over the past week were crushing me. As the perpetrator's wife, I couldn't leave my home without keeping my guard up, and the Touhin lawyers had warned me to stay at home as much as I could until things blew over.

It was only natural, of course. As a family member of the one behind the disaster, I did bear some responsibility. There may have been something his wife could have done to prevent the accident. Touhin had told the public that the accident was the result of my husband accelerating too much. But that just didn't ring true to me; he'd always been such a stickler for safety.

His father had also been a train conductor for Touhin. He'd admired his father's work ethic, and his constant refrain had been that it was his job to keep passengers safe. Touhin, in its bid to win a cutthroat war for passengers against other rail companies, had been trying to create a crammed timetable with the intention of speeding things up. But he had refused to cut corners. Due to his earnest and uncompromising nature, he never rose up the ranks within the company, and for a time, he'd even been removed from the wheel. Yet he'd never wavered in his beliefs, continuing to preach safety first until his dying day.

I was his wife. It was on me to believe in the love of my life. But on the other hand, thinking about the victims and their bereaved families stabbed me with guilt and regret.

Suddenly, the intercom rang. All the lights in the house were turned off so that it wouldn't be clear I was home. But they kept pressing the intercom button over and over again, as if to let me know they were annoyed.

"Mrs. Kitamura, you're in there, aren't you?"

It was the press.

"Could you please answer some questions about your husband, Mrs. Kitamura?"

"We've been waiting since this morning, Mrs. Kitamura. All we'd like is five minutes of your time, so could we please hear your side of the story?"

Hana, who'd been curled up on the carpet, climbed onto my lap in fear.

"Mrs. Kitamura!"

"We know you're in there, Mrs. Kitamura! Mrs. Kitamura!"

With their shouting in the background, the landline rang again. Ten rings. Twenty rings. Thirty rings. Even after forty rings, it wouldn't stop. I hugged Hana tight; it felt like the whole world had turned against me.

The harassment continued into the next day, and the next, and the next. The media mobbed my house day after day, giving my intercom no quarter, and my home phone never stopped ringing, the prank calls tormenting me well into the night.

The neighbors' reaction was especially shocking. I went to put out the trash after making sure the coast was clear of reporters, and at first, the people I met outside were kind to me, telling me I was free to ask them anything if I was ever in need. But now those people were acting strangely cold and distant. One time, some of them were openly whispering among themselves next to the garbage-dump area.

"I'm truly sorry for causing you all this trouble," I told them, bowing from a slight distance.

But they hurried away without replying. These were invariably people who'd shared meals with my husband. In fact, we'd known some of them since we started living in our home over twenty years ago. The pillars holding up my trust in others now lost, the life drained from my soul where I stood.

It happened early in the morning, about ten days after the derailment. I heard the first-floor window shatter. It didn't take much imagination to conclude somebody had thrown a rock.

Down the stairs, I found the living-room window in shards and pieces. Fearfully, I stepped outside, and when I saw it, shivers ran down my spine.

KILLER'S HOUSE

Those were the words scrawled in pink spray paint on the wall to the side of my front door. Who'd done this? The media? Somebody after a few laughs or clicks? Or had it been someone from the neighborhood?

Hana sidled up to my legs, but I was too emotionally bricked to pick her up. The future looked so dark and depressing, and I felt as petrified as a fossil.

I ascended the stairs one step at a time toward the floor where the press conference was located. While there was an elevator right next to the staircase, I decided to walk, as there was no way it'd be safe for someone in my position to use the elevator.

A briefing session for the bereaved was currently being held on the seventh floor of this large hotel. The other day, I asked the Touhin lawyers to allow me to go and apologize to the families of the deceased, but they point-blank rejected my request. They told me I wasn't allowed to come because it would complicate things. *"Please remain on standby at home."*

A short time back, I watched a documentary program about the derailment's various victims. One high school girl whose life was taken had been slated to enter nursing school in April. She'd lost her father to an illness when she was a child, and her desire to help the sick spurred her to work part-time jobs all throughout her three years of high school and save up the money to cover her tuition.

Her name was called during what would have been her high school graduation ceremony, which was held three days after the accident. Watching her friend have to receive the diploma in her place cast a pall of misery over my heart. I couldn't watch the rest of the documentary after that.

The accident had robbed that poor girl of her future. A future full of drive and ambition. And of course, it had taken the futures of her family members as well. How could anybody ever forgive us?

I arrived at the seventh floor, which had a large meeting hall called the Room of Red Leaves.

"You've *got* to be joking!" A woman was shouting on the other side of the hall's red wall. "There *is* no silver lining when an accident claims people's lives! Do you people even understand what you've done?"

I gasped. Her fury was beyond evident.

"The derailment took my beloved fiancé away from me. And his life isn't the only thing you people stole. You stole his future. His isn't the only future that's been stolen, either: *My* future's now one without him in it. Do you even realize that you've robbed the victims' loved ones of their futures? Don't just sit there! Answer me, why don't you?!"

I couldn't help but feel like her words were directed at *me*. I hastened toward the hall's entrance.

"Who're *you*?" the people at the reception desk demanded, but I broke free of them and flung open the double doors into the hall. There, I saw the bereaved sitting in rows and rows of folding chairs, with suited Touhin executives sitting in their own row opposite them. At the far left of their table, a young lawyer was there to issue constant instructions over the phone.

"Answer me! Go on, say something! Give us your answer!"

The young woman's words stabbed me right in the heart. As she walked closer to the row of suits, I stood in front of the bereaved.

"Hello, everyone… My name is Misako Kitamura, and I'm the wife of the conductor who caused the accident."

I bowed deeply; the people were abuzz now, stirring and talking.

"My late husband cannot apologize to the victims' loved ones himself, so please allow me to do so in his stead. I am so, so sorry for your loss. I'm so sorry!"

"Don't just let her do what she wants!" a voice shouted.

"Somebody drag her outta here!"

But amid all the unkind outbursts, I persisted. "Since the causes of the accident came to light and my husband was found to be in the wrong, as his wife, I intend to atone for it with my life. Please accept my humble apologies. I'm so, so sorry. I'm truly sorry for your pain!"

Before I knew it, I was on my knees. After I put my hands on the floor and bowed my head more times than I could count, I was forced back to my feet from behind. The lawyer gave me a baleful glare and grabbed my wrist tight out of naked irritation, hauling me out of the hall.

The woman who had been shouting earlier watched as I exited the room. Her eyes didn't bear the hostility the other bereaved family members' did. She wasn't staring at me with anger, but having said that, her eyes showed no forgiveness, either. They were just tremendously *sad*. They were watery and puffy; she must have cried her eyes out a great number of times since the accident. Never before had I ever witnessed a pair of eyes carrying so much sorrow.

I shook off my captor's hands and bowed in her direction. When I looked back up, I saw that the older man who had been nestled up close to that woman was bowing as deeply as I had—toward *me*. But his gentlemanly demeanor only made me feel even guiltier.

The Yoshino cherry tree in my garden was beginning to bud; its white flowers would only take a few more days to blossom fully.

In April, the petals of the blossoms gradually began to scatter. It was once my springtime routine to go out onto the road and sweep the petals together using a broom after seeing my husband off to work at the door. And spring was also the season when the neighborhood's children entered elementary school. Little kids carrying school bags for the first time would cross the road in front of my house to go to school, anxious looks on their faces. I'd always have fun watching them grow up over time. The way their expressions shifted from apprehensive to smiling after a week of entering school was a marvel.

Some of the children would even direct a *"Good morning, miss!"* my way as I swept; they must have just learned to be polite and greet others at school.

The same time a year later, of course, I'd see those children, and of course, they'd be a little taller than before. The sight of a year's worth of wear on their leather backpacks lent the kids something of an air of hardiness. As someone who didn't have any children myself, watching these children grow up was a secret pleasure of mine.

This year, however, it seemed that wouldn't be in the cards for me. Twenty whole days had passed since the accident, and yet the prank calls never ceased. And while the media was no longer besieging my home, I was still largely unable to leave my home since the eyes of my own neighborhood remained on me. The best I could manage was to cover the graffiti on my wall using a standard blue tarp in the middle of the night.

Just as March was giving way to April, the story regarding the accident began to change. With each passing day, the narrative surrounding the Touhin Railway Disaster was slipping more and more into a state of flux.

The initial explanation pinned it all on the conductor, but then people found *wrinkles*, like the stone that someone had placed on the tracks, and the defects in parts provided by a client company. All of a sudden, there was no singular explanation. Impartial investigators, including the police, uncovered that that train was in use past its service life. The company had prioritized convenience and cost cuts, and the train's components had been replaced sloppily, resulting in catastrophic brake failure. It wasn't my husband who'd gotten the train derailed.

The official report was released on April 24, fifty days following the accident. And in a peculiar twist of fate, that day just so happened to coincide with my husband's birthday.

For the first time in quite a while, a heavy breeze blew in from the open window.

I drew the yellow curtains, and the red-tinged sunlight streamed into my living room. A wooden, antique-looking rocking chair lay next to the window. My husband used to sit in that chair all the time. But that familiar fixture of my life was now gone. The sight I'd taken for granted back then was now a lost treasure in my mind.

I'd met him when I was twenty-eight years old. I'd broken my leg on the Kamakura Line platform, and he'd been the one to give me first aid. He was three years older than me, and even back then, he'd been so levelheaded that I couldn't believe he was only in his thirties. He was unwaveringly committed to his way of life. So much so that whenever he did say something, you could always believe it was entirely correct. He was a reticent man and never showy or flashy, but I was attracted by the strength at the core of him.

Ever since we got married, I'd taken to calling him "Dad"—a moniker meaning that I found him dependable. He was the shy sort, so he kept asking me to stop calling him that, but as time went by, he stopped objecting.

Although my husband had worked for Touhin for many years, back when we were newlyweds, he was bad at saluting properly. I used to laugh and tell him the way he did it looked odd. To help him improve his skills, I had him salute for me whenever the chance arose. We were about to sit down for a meal? Give me a salute. You're going to take your bath? Give me a salute. His bashful way of doing it was so endearing. Thinking back on those days made me smile.

I'd always struggled with infertility, and I knew that my husband had a great love for kids. Whenever he saw a baby at the station platform, he'd go and talk to him or her. He usually kept candy in the breast pocket of his uniform, and I'd watched him hand some out to crying children many a time.

I tried infertility treatments, but nothing seemed to work, so I ended up telling him to find another wife. He refused, though, saying that even if he couldn't have a child, that was fine by him as long as he had me. He made me stop the infertility treatments; he must not have wanted to see me suffer any further.

It happened in the early autumn of the third year of our marriage. I saw my husband drinking tea, seated at a table with a couple at a nearby coffee shop. That couple was related to us. When I entered the café to find out what that was all about, I overheard them talking about some complicated matter.

"Man, not being able to have kids? That sounds tough."

Upon hearing those words, I stopped in my tracks before reaching their table.

That couple was running their mouths about it. "Maybe you two should split up?" said one of them.

Finally, my husband spoke. "It may be rough not having kids; I can't deny that. But not once have I ever wanted a different wife. Whether or not she can have children, my wife is my wife. I love her, and that'll never change. Maybe you two should take a good look at the way you're living your own lives before you presume to take that tone with me. Now, if you'll excuse me."

My husband sprang to his feet and slammed a thousand-yen bill on the table. It was the first time I'd ever seen my normally calm husband raise his voice like that. I watched his back as he left the café without noticing me there, and in that moment, he strode like an absolute titan of a man.

As I reminisced about the time I spent with him, the tears started flowing. Everything that happened to me since the derailment left me with no time to process anything, and I had yet to properly grieve. Whenever I reached a point where I could take a breather, that was when the sorrow hit me like a tidal wave.

I never got to tend to him at his bedside, and I couldn't even hold a funeral for him to give him the send-off he deserved. Instead, we'd cremated him as furtively as we could.

Hana, who'd been out playing in the garden, slipped in through the gap in the curtains. She would reach the age of ten this year. After she was abandoned in town one rainy day, my husband had brought her home with him. Whenever he was sitting in his rocking chair, Hana would always come rest on his lap and indulge in scritches. The sight never failed to warm my heart. And now that chair would remain devoid of his presence forever.

Hana jumped into the empty rocking chair, curling up on top of the lap blanket as if longing for its former occupant's warmth. Seeing how lonely she looked made my chest seize up.

The lobby was mainly pink in color, and there were people lined up shoulder to shoulder waiting for their turn to see a doctor. The quiet "healing music" playing over the speakers throughout the hospital, designed to soothe patients' anxiety, sounded like music-box tunes.

I was paying a visit to a mental health clinic near Odawara Castle. Around the end of the Golden Week holidays, I started noticing worrying changes in my body, like my right hand shaking when I tried holding my chopsticks, or losing my ability to keep track of time while soaking in the bathtub and noticing that almost an hour had passed upon snapping back to reality.

Moreover, whenever I stepped outside, everything in my line of sight had started feeling *false* somehow. Figuring these were no passing symptoms, I searched for a local clinic on my smartphone. This place was a full-fledged mental health clinic that dealt in psychiatry and psychosomatic medicine, as well as memory disorders for patients with dementia.

"Mrs. Kitamura, could you kindly fill out this form and wait here? Thank you."

A young nurse handed me a medical questionnaire as I sat on a sofa in the lobby. The sheet in the clipboard contained as many as thirty questions. Was I sleeping well at night? Was I eating three square meals a day?

I filled it in, and it felt like my trembling hands were thrusting in my face the fact that my body was acting up. Since the derailment, I hadn't gone a day without waking up in the middle of the night, and I'd lost almost ten kilograms. I received a shock this morning when I looked at myself in the mirror; I had noticeably more gray hairs, and my gaunt and pallid face lacked any radiance. It didn't even register as my own face at first.

"It'll be okay. I'll be here by your side the whole time."

An elderly couple had returned to the lobby from a small room in the back following a medical evaluation. The husband had his arm locked in his wife's, propping her up. She had a brooding expression on her face.

"No worries, honey, no worries."

"Thank you, dear."

The man who'd always been there to lend me a shoulder whenever I felt unwell was no longer with me. Back when I was undergoing those infertility treatments, my husband would rush to the bathroom to rub my back when I was vomiting. He'd wipe my dirty mouth for me without ever betraying a disgusted look. But now the man who'd always been by my side was no longer in this world.

When I stood up to hand in the completed questionnaire, I felt dizzy on my feet. My heart contracted, and I collapsed back onto the sofa.

"Are you okay?!"

Disconcerted, the old man sitting next to me leaned in close.

"I'm so sorry. I'm fine—please don't worry about me."

With time, the pain in my chest subsided. I also told the nurse who'd rushed to my side that I was okay.

The old man stared at me, concern in his eyes. "Are you *sure* you're okay, ma'am?"

"Yes, I'm sure. I just got a little dizzy from standing up too fast."

The old man looked me over, and then he got to his feet, heading to the watercooler by the bathroom, and he brought me a paper cup of water.

"Here—if you need it."

"Thank you very much. I could use some water."

He flashed me a reassuring smile.

"Mr. Ujiki," said the receptionist, "please come into the examination room in the back."

"Looks like I'm wanted." He smiled once more before entering the dementia clinic.

Sipping the cold water, I could feel it travel down my body and bring moisture back to it. The pent-up emotions in my heart, on the other hand, didn't likewise vanish.

Stored in one of the drawers of our living room closet was an album containing photos I'd taken with my husband. He was shy, so he didn't like being photographed, but I captured him on camera whenever I got the chance. I knew that someday, when I was older, it'd be good to have the photos as mementos, and I reckoned anything that aided in having strong recollections of eras past would give us the courage to keep on living.

Thanks to the prescription I received at the mental clinic, I was able to sleep to some extent at night. I took the thick album from inside the drawer and flipped through the pages one by one. There, a photo from our honeymoon in Hokkaido. Here, a photo of the three of us on the day we adopted Hana. There, a photo of the *yakiniku* party we'd held in our garden.

A photo of us as newlyweds made me smile. He was standing in uniform, saluting shyly. This picture was taken when I went to the platform of Nishi-Yugawara Station to deliver the bento he'd forgotten at home. Even though other people could see, I had him give me another practice salute. He got all indignant. *"C'mon, stop. Not in a place like this…"* But after I insisted, he did it for me, though reluctantly.

In the midpoint of the album, there were pages containing particularly large photos. More than one such photo was taken during our anniversary celebration at a restaurant in Minami-Kamakura. The restaurant gave customers a commemorative photo at the end of their meal. We'd visited the restaurant every year since the year we got married, and it became our tradition to include those photos in the album. I'd already made the latest reservation at that restaurant the day after my anniversary celebration last year. This year, I was scheduled to get our twenty-fourth such photo taken a week from today, on May 19. Every year, I told him the following over our multicourse anniversary meal.

"The year either one of us departs this life, let the other come to this place alone. I think drinking some wine while reminiscing about your spouse isn't the worst idea."

He just grimaced and told me not to talk about such morbid stuff. And now that reality had befallen us. For the last week or so, I'd been wondering whether I ought to cancel our reservation. I did feel like going alone. Perhaps a sip or two of my favorite red would buoy my spirits a little. But would the world tolerate the idea of the wife of the conductor who caused the accident spending her anniversary someplace special?

As I was sitting in my chair, deep in thought, the intercom rang. I looked outside through the gap in the curtains and saw an unfamiliar wheelchair-bound woman before the gate. The air about her told me she wasn't with the media.

Suspicious though I was, I pressed the button. "Yes?"

"Is this Mr. Kitamura's wife?" she asked.

"It is. Can I help you?"

"I'm so sorry to bother you in the middle of the day like this. My name is Ishida; I run a restaurant in Odawara. I owe your dearly departed husband a great deal, so I thought I'd come give his wife my condolences."

I could sense the compassion in the voice the intercom carried to me. Her every word was dripping with decency and humility. I opened the front door slowly, and when I saw the look on her face, any suspicions I might have had instantly disappeared. The sincerity I'd heard in her voice was plain to see on her face as well.

I walked over and opened the gate, and the white-haired woman bowed deeply from her wheelchair.

"Again, my name is Ishida. I know it's rude of me to pay you a visit when you have the weight of the accident on your heart. Please forgive me. And please forgive my rudeness for asking for your address secondhand as well."

"Oh, no, thank you so much for going out of your way to visit me. By all means, come in." I beckoned her inside.

"Thank you, but here's okay. As you can see, my legs are failing me." Then she started talking about my husband. "I boarded the train using Odawarajou-mae Station, and I would have to contact the station and ask for assistance. And it was always Mr. Kitamura who helped me. He always waited until I was situated inside the train before he started it again, and that didn't change even when some kind of trouble was causing delays. He'd interrupt the complaining passengers and provide for me with kindness and respect."

I remained silent.

"He's actually waited for me in front of the station so he could push me onto the train himself. And when the station received a call from me, he'd even wake up during his between-rides nap and wait for me at the bottom of the stairs."

That sounds like him all right. I could picture it. Him pushing her wheelchair.

"Mr. Kitamura would always speak the world of you."

"What?"

"He said you'd always get up with him no matter how early it was in the morning and see him off at the front door. And that no matter how many times he told you you didn't need to do that for him, you always insisted. He told me that your wishing him a good day every day gave him the strength to put in another day's hard work."

I said nothing.

"I've lost my husband as well, so we spoke of our spouses often. Some time ago, Mr. Kitamura told me that if he were to be reborn, he'd want to be with you again. I think he loved you with all his heart."

I felt a gushing of warmth in the bottom of my heart. He was shy and didn't talk much, so he'd never said *I love you* to me.

Mrs. Ishida gifted me some *katsudon* in a plastic container before leaving. According to her, it was her restaurant's specialty.

What she'd told me stuck inside my mind after I returned to the living room. The album on the table was still open to the page bearing the anniversary photo from the year prior. After listening to Mrs. Ishida's story, this photo had taken on a different shade.

But I mustn't forget. Even though my husband hadn't been at fault, the crash still resulted in the deaths of so many passengers. The pain that the bereaved families had been going through vastly outweighed my own. I could hardly disregard them by kicking back and enjoying some wine. If my husband was in my shoes, he'd never do such a thing. I gently closed the album and called the restaurant to cancel.

I washed my face, relying on the scant early-morning light trickling into the bathroom. I didn't turn on any of the lights in the house, and as the days passed, I became more and more afraid of bright places. It wasn't to prevent the media from learning I was home. Not anymore. Because at this point, brightly lit spaces were plain frightening in and of themselves to me. And that was especially the case when I woke up early in the morning to go to the bathroom.

Whenever it was too bright, I could catch sight of my rapidly aging face in the mirror. Over the past two months, I'd gotten so much more wrinkled that makeup was no longer enough to conceal it.

When I went outside to breathe in some of the crisp morning air, I heard a rustling from the mailbox next to my gate. Hana, who had woken up earlier than I had, was pawing at a pair of envelopes from her perch on the cherry-blossom branches.

She jumped nimbly down, carrying the two letters in her mouth. One was an envelope from Touhin regarding my husband's work-related accident. When I eased it out of Hana's mouth to check the envelope's contents, the other envelope fell to the ground. I picked it up and read the unfamiliar name written on the back: *Shinji Nemoto*.

Impulsively, I opened the envelope on the spot, carefully pulling what turned out to be a folded-up letter.

Dear Mrs. Misako Kitamura,

My name was written at the top. My eyes darted across the page as I read the carefully handwritten text. It was addressed to me by the one of the derailment victims' families.

Dear Mrs. Misako Kitamura,

Please forgive the suddenness of this letter. My name is Shinji Nemoto. I lost my only son, Shin'ichirou, to the accident that occurred on March 5 of this year. When we lost our beloved boy, me, my wife, and our daughter-in-law-to-be didn't know which way to turn.

I'm sure you remember the briefing for the victims held on March 19. We all saw how you bowed repeatedly before the bereaved on that day. That's not something just anybody has the courage to do under those circumstances. It made clear just how exceedingly sincere and honest a person you are.

Ever since then, you've occupied a corner of my mind. I, too, live in Odawara. After the release of the official report on April 24, I found out your address by means of an acquaintance, as I personally wanted to convey a few words to you on the part of the bereaved. Please forgive me if I'm overstepping, but I felt compelled to write you. I sincerely apologize for any inconvenience.

First of all, I learned through various media outlets that you've been tormented in several ways by heartless and cruel individuals, and that breaks my heart. They're too cowardly to be able to apologize to your face, so please allow me to do so in their stead. I'm truly sorry.

Next, regarding the derailment: Conductor Takao Kitamura is not at fault in any way, shape, or form, to say nothing of you, his wife. You bear no responsibility whatsoever. During the coming trial, if the actual wrongdoers, Touhin Railway, cause you even the smallest bit of trouble, I will take the stand as a witness. Again, I must stress that you are not responsible.

That day at the victim-briefing session, I saw how you had the same look in your eyes as my daughter-in-law. You lost your beloved husband in this accident. In your eyes, I saw a form of sorrow and grief that can only be found in someone who has cried and cried and cried some more.

Mrs. Kitamura, I believe that people have the right to end their lives by their own hands. The idea that a total stranger can interfere with the right we all possess is a daft one. That being said, please take this as a rule of thumb from someone who's pushing seventy years old.

Mrs. Kitamura. You mustn't die. You mustn't.

Life is marked by many slopes, some a climb up and some a tumble down, but it's my conviction that life is nonetheless worth living.

This month, our daughter-in-law learned she is pregnant. The father is, of course, my son. My Shin'ichirou.

Our family has chosen the path of life. And just as the steepest downhill slopes must eventually level off, this world will always offer us a future that's full of light.

Life is a funny thing. I pray that one day, a dazzling and beautiful light will be cast on your future.

Have faith.

Have faith, and believe.

Shinji Nemoto
Taeko Nemoto
Tomoko Nemoto

His words spoke to me, and tears rolled down my cheeks. The three names written at the end each had different handwriting. Each of the three members of his family had essentially added their signature, affirming that these were not the opinions of Shinji Nemoto alone. His wife and his daughter-in-law must have given the text a pass as well. This letter was a letter from the whole Nemoto family.

Elementary school students with their telltale leather backpacks strolled in front of my cherry tree. A girl whose backpack was red smiled at me as I stood in front of my gate.

"Morning, miss!"

The other kids took that as their cue, coming up from behind and beaming at me.

"Good morning!" they said. "Morning, ma'am!"

These were the same children who'd taken this route to school in early spring last year. Everyone had gotten a smidgen taller, and their faces looked a little more grown-up.

"…Good morning, everyone." My tears were streaming into my quivering lip. "Good morning! Morning, everyone! Morning!"

I couldn't look depressed before the children's eyes. They had futures ahead of them. So I shouted cheerily.

Hana sidled up to my legs, and I picked her up and wiped my wet eyes with the palm of my hand.

I walked along the tracks; the station platform looked empty. With no trains running, the area was totally silent. That fact, coupled with the setting sun, lent the area around Nishi-Yuigahama Station a gloomy atmosphere.

Holding a bouquet of flowers wrapped in cellophane, I headed to my destination. Walking around outside was a rare event for me since the crash. My face was a bit stiff; leaving my home for the first time in a while had me nervous. The location was along the railroad tracks but far from the station platform. When I reached it, I saw a large number of flower arrangements stacked one on top of the other, with chrysanthemums at the center.

March 5, 11:29 AM. This was where that Touhin Railway rapid train derailed. My husband was killed instantly. This very spot was where he'd drawn his last breath.

"Hi, Dad. I'm here. I made it."

I peeled away the cellophane and placed down the chrysanthemums.

"I'm sorry," I said, straining my voice. "Forgive me for taking so long."

I was choked with emotion. When we held the small service for my husband, I had been unable to truly say my good-byes properly, not least because of the suddenness of everything that had happened. Now that I was visiting this place after so much time had passed since the accident, something was darkening the doorstep of my heart.

A little farther along the railroad tracks stood a man who had his hands together in prayer like I did. He'd placed a bouquet on the ground by his feet, his eyes closed and a solemn look on his face. My gaze met the old man's as he slowly opened his eyes. When I gave him a slight bow, it dawned on me that his was a face I recognized. He was the man who'd fetched me some water at the mental clinic. Mr. Ujiki, I believed his name was.

He remembered me, too; he walked over to me and smiled. "Are you feeling okay now?" he asked.

"Thanks to your kindness, I'm feeling a little better."

"I'm happy to hear that… By the way," he said hesitantly, glancing at the flowers piled up by him, "I don't mean to pry, but did you lose someone in the Kamakura Line disaster?"

After a slight pause, I nodded.

"I'm truly sorry for asking such a personal question."

I shook my head. "Don't worry about it, sir."

He bowed apologetically before standing back up and shifting his gaze to the tracks. In his gaunt face, I caught a glimpse of the cloud hanging over him, and it was the same type as my own. I couldn't help but think he was putting up something of a brave front.

"Please forgive the intrusion, but could it be that you also lost someone to the crash?"

For a moment, Mr. Ujiki remained silent. He heaved a sorrowful sigh and hung his head.

"Last February, my granddaughter leaped in front of the rapid train here. After she got sent flying by the impact, she was found by the torii gate of that there Kamakura Ikitama Shrine, barely recognizable..."

I was at a loss for words. While the circumstances differed, we'd both lost loved ones. My heart hurt for him, because it really felt like his pain was my own. He must have taken everything to do with his granddaughter's death on himself. Given the seriousness of the subject, he couldn't talk about it off-handedly. All the greasy sweat on his forehead was enough to tell me how much darkness he was harboring in his soul.

"If you don't mind, would you like to talk about it?" I asked him, gently clasping his hands in mine.

If he got the chance to express to someone the pain he was in, it'd ease that pain a little. I, too, knew the pain of not being able to talk to anybody about the crash.

"Thank you... Thank you very much." His stiff expression relaxed out of gratitude. He looked up at the sky, and then the dam burst, and it all came out. "You see, my granddaughter—she was bullied mercilessly at school. But she never talked to anybody about it. She was raised by a single mother, although her mother was so busy with work that she can't really be said to have raised her. From my granddaughter's perspective, she must've thought confiding in her would've been pointless. To me, she was my one and only beloved granddaughter. So why didn't she come to *me* about the bullying? And more than anything, why oh why did I never realize what was going on? I'll never stop kicking myself over that. She was strong-willed, but she was just *such* a kindhearted girl. Could it be that she didn't come talk to me about it because she didn't want me to worry after I started going to the nursing center? The suicide note found in one of the drawers in her room was very short. It was a single sentence. It read, 'Man cannot trust in anyone.'"

He averted his gaze, an expression of supreme sorrow on his face. But then he lifted his voice, speaking more sharply. "I'd have liked her to learn to trust in her fellow human beings. And I'd have liked her to see the other side of the coin. There's malice, yes, but there's also goodness so strong, it encompasses all."

The bloodred sunset began to tinge the town, eating away at the pressing darkness.

"I'm suffering from dementia. It won't be long before I lose all my memories. But my memories of her, I never want to lose. Never. I refuse to!" he averred to me and to himself. He took out a bunch of notebooks from the leather bag he carried on his shoulder. "I'll fight to remember my granddaughter's name. That's why I keep writing her name in my notebooks every day. It's so I carve it deep into my mind. No matter how many thousands or tens of thousands of times I have to write it."

I could see one name written over and over on every page of the notebook, leaving no white space: *Yukiho*.

"Of course," he continued as he basked in the red sun's light, "forgetting people who gave you so many memories isn't that easy. Or am I wrong?"

His words pierced me right in the heart. I bit my lip hard thinking about my husband. I could never forget him.

Hana was curled up in the living room, atop the rocking chair. She seemed to think my husband would return to his chair someday. Whenever she heard a noise outside, she'd rush out the door thinking he must have finally come home. When she trudged back inside with that forlorn expression in her eyes, I could hardly bear to look. I did contemplate getting rid of the chair. Maybe it'd mean I thought about him less. And maybe it'd make it so that Hana stopped keeping her hopes up. But I couldn't do it. It felt like he was still in that chair, somehow. Like someday, he'd casually come back in and take a seat there. It stung every time I saw it, but I couldn't bring myself to throw it out regardless.

I heard a car stop outside the gate of my home. And I heard the *clank* of something metal being unloaded from the car's load tray.

"Hello, miss? We're with Yugawara Builders!"

Hana jumped out of the rocking chair; she must've figured my husband was back. I picked her up before she could reach the front door and exited the living room to let them in.

"Thank you for your help. Please come right in."

The two men in work clothes entered. In order to remove the graffiti on the wall, I'd searched for help online and turned to a building contractor company based in the next town over. I'd told them in advance that my husband was the conductor who'd died in the Kamakura Line crash, hence the graffiti.

After some words of greeting, the two men stood side by side and bowed their heads. "We're very sorry for your loss, ma'am."

I felt humbled by their courteousness.

"Also, ma'am, while I didn't know if I should tell you," said the young man on the right, who was shooting me a meaningful look, "I also lost someone to the Kamakura Line derailment. My father."

A wave rippled inside my chest.

"Yuuichi, I'll go work on the wall."

The gray-haired man standing next to him walked outside. He must have sensed the young man and I would be getting into it.

Yuuichi gave him an apologetic look. "Sorry about this, Mr. Takenaka."

"I see," I said. "I'm so sorry I made such an insensitive request of you. I had no idea you had to face such a thing."

I put Hana back onto the floor and bowed my head deeply.

"Oh, no, ma'am, it's nothing to apologize for," he replied, gently placing a hand on my upper arm. "Please raise your head. Not to state the obvious, but I don't have any grudge against your husband. Not at all. I don't bear a single crumb of resentment, so no need for any concern or consideration. Just allow us to do what we do best."

He flashed me a reassuring smile and started stroking Hana on the head. "Who's a good kitty? You are!"

Then his expression suddenly tensed up. "By the way, Mrs. Kitamura, there's something I really need to talk to you about… If you could see your husband one more time, would you?"

I didn't understand what he was getting at.

"What I'm about to tell you is a hundred-percent true. It's not some joke, I swear. If you go to Nishi-Yuigahama Station in the middle of the night, a ghost will appear on the platform. A phantom train runs down the Kamakura Line tracks, and you can board the train that derailed on that day. I myself went there and met with my father."

He said all this wild stuff without halting or stumbling over his words.

"If, ever since the crash, you've found yourself stuck in one place and unable to move forward, you should go see the man you love one last time. The watch I'm wearing is the one my father was wearing when the train derailed. He and I exchanged words on the ghost train. I repaired the watch, which the accident broke, and after I decided to wear it in memory of him..." He looked at me without averting his gaze. "Time started moving forward for me again."

The sky stretching above the station was bluish-black. The electronic noticeboard was off, and darkness shrouded the platform, at the very back of which was an area illuminated by the scant moonlight. And someone was standing there, right by the yellow tactile paving, as if to bask in the spotlight. Looking closely, I saw she was a young woman wearing a sailor-style school uniform. She was holding a small pink conch shell, staring at it with solemn eyes. Did she have some sort of attachment to that shell? I started walking toward her.

She turned to look at me. "I wonder if you'll end up being the last passenger."

"I'm sorry, but might you be a ghost?"

"Indeed I am. Surprised?"

I was. Yuuichi hadn't specified what gender the ghost was. I'd been expecting a scarier male apparition.

"The fact that you're here at this hour means you heard about the phantom train, right?" she asked.

I simply straightened up in silence.

"Good, you already know half of it." And then she laid out the four rules for boarding the train.

* * *

- You may board the train only from the station where the doomed rider first boarded.
- You mustn't tell the doomed rider that they are soon to die.
- You must get off the train at or before passing Nishi-Yuigahama Station. Otherwise, you, too, shall die in the accident.
- Meeting the doomed rider will not change their fate. No matter what you do, those who died in the accident will not come back to life. If you attempt to get people off the train before it derails, you will be returned to the present day.

"If you can follow the rules I created, then get on that train. Oh, speak of the devil."

After she quickly rattled off her rules, she gave me a grin. She pointed with her eyes at the black, see-through train that was fast approaching.

My heart jumped when I saw the train stop right before our eyes. My husband was there. He was *there*, in the conductor's cab.

"Dad...," I said. My funny little nickname for him.

As I held my hand over my mouth in shock, the train slowly began to depart. A few minutes later, an ear-piercing roar rumbled from a distance down the tracks.

She went on and on through my confusion. "The train that just passed us by is the very same train that crashed on that day. And Rule Number Three is the honest truth. If you don't get off the train before it crashes, that'll be what becomes of you, too. This ghost train is only visible to those with strong emotional ties to the accident. But soon, nobody will be able to see it anymore. On May twenty-eighth, the day after tomorrow, the safety inspection of the Kamakura Line will come to a close, and trains will start running down the line starting from the first morning departure on that day. Do you get what I'm driving at?"

I said nothing.

"Long story short, the ghost train that appears late tomorrow night will be the last one. If you're going to board the train, tomorrow's your last chance."

I took slow, deep breaths to calm my nerves and compose myself. I had to process this information. Of course, I wasn't going to hesitate to do it. Sure, meeting him again wouldn't bring him back to life in reality, but that did nothing to deter me. I would board the final train, and I would see my husband again.

It was a chilly night. So chilly, it was hard to believe it was late May. Above the platform, the stars twinkled like a cloud of gold dust. Maybe it was the clearness of the air, but the starry sky felt strangely close.

Making use of the starlight, I checked my clothes in the mirror on the platform wall. I was wearing a lavender cardigan I'd bought right before last year's anniversary. There was no way I was going to spend my last-ever time with my husband in some unseemly ensemble. While I looked a tad emaciated, I still looked nice and stylish in my own way, if I did say so myself. What's more, it was the first time I'd put on some nice makeup since the accident.

Suddenly, light illuminated the reflection I was looking at in the mirror. Surprised, I turned around, and I found the electronic noticeboard was now on:

RAPID TRAIN
MINAMI-KAMAKURA   10:26

The black translucent train was now approaching the platform. It was significantly more transparent than the night before, as if to tell me this was well and truly its last ride.

The train came to a halt, and I spotted him in uniform in the conductor's cab. He was conscientiously checking all the equipment with a serious expression on his face. In order to avoid his gaze, I boarded via Car One, through the door closest to Car Two.

"The Minami-Kamakura–bound train will be departing from Nishi-Yugawara Station momentarily," came my husband's announcement.

I walked up to his compartment. All the doors inside the car closed at once.

Having arrived before the conductor's cabin, I bowed my head deeply to all the passengers. The people on this train would die in an hour, and as the wife of the conductor in charge of it, it was incumbent upon me to express my appreciation of their lives.

I slowly straightened back up and grabbed onto one of the ceiling straps next to me before casting a glance at the nearby conductor's compartment.

My husband was completely unaware I was on board. He was sitting behind a windowed partition, his eyes fixed on the speedometer and his hands glued to the steering wheel with a serious expression on his face. And for my part, I'd never had any intention of exchanging words with him to begin with. This being our last time together notwithstanding, I could never get in the way of his work. All I needed was to be by his side. Just watching him from up close made me sufficiently happy.

When we arrived at Enoura Station, passengers rushed in through the doors. A man who appeared to be an office worker wearing a suit was holding a paper bag with the word *Hakodate* written on it. Was he perhaps planning to give the colleagues at his office some nice souvenir snacks from that port in Hokkaido?

We'd honeymooned in Hokkaido. Seven months after our wedding, we visited Hakodate in the winter. But I'd had a cold, one I inadvertently passed on to him while on the plane. As soon as we checked into their hotel in Hakodate, we both started hacking and coughing.

Originally, we'd planned to have dinner at the sushi restaurant we'd booked for the first day of our trip. But since he figured walking out in the frigid air could exacerbate our colds, we ended up having dinner in our hotel room instead. We sat across from each other using the chairs by the window, and there, we ate the thing of frozen crab fried rice we ordered via room service. We thought we could make the most of it by looking out on what was sure to be a beautiful nightscape, but the heavy snow that had begun to fall made it impossible to get a view outside the window.

"We came all the way to Hokkaido, and look at us now," I'd said.

He chuckled, and it was contagious because I burst into laughter. Fortunately, we both felt better by the next morning. That evening, we visited the sushi restaurant we'd missed out on the day before. And we also got to enjoy the night view of Hakodate. The next morning, we hit Noboribetsu and soaked in some lovely hot springs. However, whenever I reminisced about our honeymoon, the first memory that sprang to mind was us eating that frozen crab fried rice together by the window.

"Wow, this fried rice is surprisingly good, huh?" he'd said with a smile.

At that moment, I thought that really, it was the little things like this that made married life what it was. And it was also the moment I knew for sure I could go on like this forever, so long as I was with him.

The train passed Odawarajou-mae Station before pulling into Maekawa Station. I saw old wooden benches out the window. The charming and refined atmosphere hadn't changed since the olden days.

Twenty-six years ago, he and I met for the first time on this very platform. Back then, I'd been living near Maekawa Station. One day, I went to the station wearing high heels and ended up badly spraining my right foot as I passed through the ticket gate. He found me seated on a platform bench, immobilized.

"What's the matter, miss?"

He put a splint on my foot and administered some first aid. As he bandaged it, a gust of wind blew, and the worn-out cap of his uniform, with its frayed visor and all, went flying away.

"Ah, your hat!"

But he wasn't going anywhere. "Don't move," he urged, continuing his careful work bandaging my foot. The cap fell onto the tracks and subsequently got trampled over by an oncoming express train.

One week after that day, I spotted him on the platform of Maekawa Station again, and he was wearing a new cap to go with his uniform.

I bowed and said, "Thank you very much for the other day."

"Don't mention it," he replied, his expression softening.

One day, after we got married, I found a tattered cap stored in his desk drawer. It was all but torn to shreds. It was clear to see that it got run over by some vehicle, which could only mean it was the very same cap he'd lost the day he gave me first aid. He'd gone down to the tracks afterward to retrieve it. The cap had been worn by his father before him, and when he himself became a conductor, he'd started donning it in order to follow his father's last wishes. In other words, he hadn't batted an eye at the wind blowing away that memento of his father so he could keep helping me with my injury.

Every memory warmed my heart. As I held on to the strap, I cast my thoughts to days long past.

Before I knew it, the train had passed Koiso Station. As I turned my attention to the operator's cab, my gaze met his through the door window. He shot me a confused look: *Why are you here?* But then he turned back to the controls in order to slow the train down as it pulled into Chigasaki Kaigan Station. He calmly and dispassionately went about his duties without turning to look at me.

As he was so serious and straight-laced, I reckoned he wouldn't turn to look at me a second time. I was just glad that I could finally make eye contact with him, even if it was for but a fleeting moment.

The train had now passed Enoshima. There wasn't much time left. The coast of Sagami Bay came into view through the window as the train sped mercilessly onward.

We were at Yuigahama now. He and I had paid Yuigahama Beach a visit before on one cold December day. I was in low spirits after stopping my infertility treatments, and he drove us to the beach as a change of pace. With the sun above setting on the horizon, he and I were sitting right on the sand, gazing from a short distance away as the water came and went, came and went. He'd been silent the entire time, until suddenly, he spoke.

"I'm sorry I couldn't do anything for you."

There was nothing I could say to that. It was hardly *his* fault that I couldn't bear children. But since as a couple, we always supported each other, he still felt some measure of responsibility over it.

"Daddy!"

A small child ran down the stairs leading to the beach. He dashed past us, chasing after his father. A mother appeared from behind, a baby in her arms. The family of four gathered on the water's edge, chatting lightheartedly.

The family unit was so dazzling to me. I turned my eyes away from the sea; I couldn't bear to look back up again. My husband put his arm around my shoulders and pulled my body closer to him. He wasn't usually the type to be this bold, but he didn't hesitate to embrace me. His weight on my shoulders was an expression of his love for me; he didn't have to say anything. Tears welled up in my eyes.

"*Dad…*"

I cried into his chest. He remained silent and didn't pull his arm back.

I'd started calling him "Dad" as a show of how dependable I thought he was. He initially hated it, but after a certain point, he stopped minding. And looking back, it occurred to me that the reason he accepted being called "Dad" was because I was infertile.

Many wives took to calling their husbands "Dad" once they gave birth to a child. Maybe he thought that since I couldn't have children of our own, he'd at least let me call him a father. There was no way to ever know for sure, but considering his abiding kindness, I couldn't help but entertain the possibility.

The train was quickly decelerating. We'd soon be arriving at Nishi-Yuigahama Station. I intended to stay on the train. I couldn't let him go into the beyond alone. I'd boarded this ghost train expecting to die.

I'd placed my suicide note on the table in the living room, and I'd left Hana in Mrs. Ishida's care, calling her restaurant to feed her a story that I was going on a trip for a change of scenery. She was happy to take Hana, and I was sure she'd give Hana a happy home after I died.

The shaking of the train gradually subsided. The wheels slowed to a halt in front of a sign that read, Nishi-Yuigahama.

I didn't move from that spot. I let go of the ceiling strap and took a deep breath. The moment I slowly exhaled to compose myself, the cabin door swung open. Much to my surprise, he stepped out of the conductor's compartment.

"Get off," he said, his expression solemn but gentle.

I didn't understand.

"Get off for me. Please."

I said nothing.

"I'm sorry, Misako. I'm truly sorry…but please keep on living. For my sake."

His voice was wavering. But he was glaring at me to leave, and that pointed look made me get off in spite of myself.

"But why…?" I said.

I was standing motionless, watching as my husband returned to the conductor's compartment.

"Good work, lady."

I turned to look. It was her—the ghost girl I'd met the night before. Before I knew it, the platform was shrouded in the darkness of the night once more.

"What do you mean?" I asked.

"It's true that one of the conditions I laid out for riding this train was that you mustn't tell the doomed they're about to die. I didn't, however, say that they aren't aware of their impending deaths. They already know. They *know* they're about to die in a crash."

I just stared at her in blank amazement. She continued:

"The passengers on this ghost train are lingering souls who have yet to find peace and enter the next world. They remember their own deaths. They get on the train with their memories of the derailment intact. But ghosts are ghosts. The accident will happen no matter what they do, and reality won't change."

I couldn't wrap my head around it. *He knew? He knew the whole time he was going to die?*

"Why didn't you tell us the passengers already knew?"

"Good question. I'm not really sure why I didn't, but maybe I was thinking that the train ride would be more pleasant that way."

I didn't respond.

"I used to think that living in a world like *this* was pointless. But it seems I was mistaken. Since the derailment, so many people who heard about the ghost-train rumors have boarded this train. But not a single one of them stayed on past Nishi-Yuigahama Station. Or to be precise, they couldn't. Some among them did *try* to stay on, just like you, but their loved ones never failed to make them get off. Occasionally, their loved ones even resorted to hitting them and *forcing* them off. I mean, normally, you'd think at least one of them would, out of loneliness, be okay with their living loved one joining them in the world of souls. But no, not one of them was like that. They instead made the ones they loved choose life over death. And to me, that's beautiful."

She exhaled audibly and grasped her pink spiral seashell tightly before saying, "If I'd known that people could be this beautiful, I wouldn't have chosen death, either. Bye, then."

With a shy smile on her face, she boarded the ghost train. The doors closed quickly thereafter, as if they'd been waiting for the last passenger to arrive.

The night breeze blew once more, as if singling me out, and it lifted my bangs, carrying the scent of the sea to my nostrils.

It was time to say good-bye to my husband.

At first, I thought I couldn't allow myself to look at my husband in his conductor's room. Yes, the fault lay with the rail company, but as the wife of the conductor who'd caused the accident, I did bear some responsibility. All the people who died in the disaster were now gathered on the train in front of me. I couldn't say a proper farewell to my husband in front of those people. Perhaps he was of the same opinion now, because he wasn't turning to look at me.

I bowed deeply to the passengers on the ghost train. The moment I raised my head, I glanced once, just once, at the conductor's cab, even though I knew I shouldn't.

His shoulders were trembling.

The train slowly started moving again. Then he looked my way. He gave me a smile and a salute. It was that lousy, awkward-looking salute we practiced together a long time ago. And his smile was the childlike smile he used to flash me back then, too.

A tear rolled down my cheek. I covered my mouth, but I couldn't hold it back anymore, and I started sobbing intensely.

The ghost train derailed. It rose off the tracks and started ascending skyward, slowly weaving its way through the stars up above.

Dad... Dad...

Through the deluge of emotions, I looked up at the skies and said:

"Have a great day."